People Who
Hate America

PEOPLE WHO HATE AMERICA

Copyright © 2014 by Kim MacQueen

Champlain Books

a division of Barnes | MacQueen Publishing Resources
47 Maple St., Suite 206, Burlington, Vermont 05401
www.ChamplainBooks.com
www.barnesmacqueen.com

Printed in the United States of America
ISBN-13: 978-0-9884523-8-1
First Edition: August 2014
Library of Congress Control Number: 2014938054

Cover design by Martin Simpson

The author is alone is solely responsible for the content of this book and bears all responsibility for any claims arising from the publication of the book.

This is a work of fiction based on real events in Newark, New Jersey between 1965 and 1969. Some names and identifying details have been changed to protect the privacy of individuals.

For Steve MacQueen, Claire MacQueen and Rose MacQueen

Summer 1966

I

The thing about it was, Gloria wasn't even Italian. She grew up the only child to Irish immigrants Jane and Thomas Mallon, born in Fall 1920 on Rose Street in Newark's Central Ward, just as the trees outside the tenements lost their leaves. Same place as her husband, Hugh, and his four brothers and sisters. Same place as her husband's mother, Livia, hulking in her housedress, aerating her family's apartment with thyme and tomato smells, responding with outstretched arms and yelling to even the quietest question. Now here in midlife, at home in suburban Jersey, 30 years married into a big family from Naples, Gloria looked Italian, was even starting to feel it.

She'd spent a silent adolescence poring over European fashion magazines and a young adulthood walking up the street to work at Entwhistle's dress shop, where a small smile would always suffice in place of any actual conversation with customers. There just wasn't a need to raise your voice or express yourself with your hands the way all the Italians always did. But as she got older, her limbs heavier and harder to pull around all day, the children growing in size and number so that they were always everywhere, she sometimes had to yell to be heard above the din. Now Gloria was far enough into her 40s that she'd stopped counting, and there were days she'd start waving her arms around and putting her face in her hands almost involuntarily, as if reminding herself she was still in the room.

There weren't that many mirrors in the new house, a two-story Colonial on a monied, leafy New Shrewsbury street. But sometimes, say while she gathered laundry, she'd catch herself in the full-length oval mirror in the bedroom. In the summer she'd wear floral cotton dresses and pleated beige vamp shoes meant for the city even though she'd stay in the house all day, alone but for the youngest children. She'd stop, appraise the dress; she had so many, all so beautiful, arranged by color in the closet. But she rarely looked up, at her face. She'd have seen wavy blackish-brown hair growing out of its smart style, tucked behind her ears, needing attention. Small, light blue eyes set in the type of face people called patrician. Regal. But tired. Always tired.

And the children didn't look look half Italian/half Irish, not at all. They looked Italian, their skin faint olive against their mother's white, their eyes big and brown, all of them: two teenaged daughters, four younger sons: Marion, Lois, Victor, Anthony, Hugo Jr., Robert.

Now Gloria stood stirring a thin pot of sauce, because all of them were always hungry, all the time. She looked down into it and wondered vaguely what it needed. Livia would know without tasting it, without even smelling it, but Livia was not here now, thank God. Livia was having her hair done down the street at Ricky Lovano's with some elderly friends, her mother-in-law bedroom upstairs, spotless in her absence, as though the children's dirt stopped at her door. Their toys and books and clothes were everywhere else, the mud from their shoes in the hallway and crumbs from their breakfasts on the table, but they never went into Livia's room, as though the cross on her wall and tiny Jesus picture set carefully on the bureau doily were talismans warding all that away.

So Gloria cooked all day long, her kitchen full of canned tomatoes and spaghetti in boxes because when she went down to the market, she was never really sure what else she should buy. She'd sent Marion around the corner for Chinese takeout twice in the last two weeks. The boys didn't care, just shoved chow mein into their hungry boy gullets whenever she put it in front of them, but Lois and Marion, discerning teenagers now, had started to revolt, pushing their plates away and looking back at her with imploring eyes.

"I like it better when Grandma cooks," Marion said as Gloria set her plate down on the table the last time. "Grandma really likes to cook."

Gloria sat down that night in front of her daughter, at fourteen a hormonal force like a fan on high, and found she didn't have the energy to even respond. So she kept cooking, and the scent of the sauce took her back to walking by the Addonizios' house thirty years before. They lived on Bergen, the only Italian family in the neighborhood smack in the middle of the Irish Ward, where the air was heavy with meat and potatoes served with no spices ever, except for salt. But in front of the Addonizios' house smelled like sausage and thyme. To Gloria it smelled wild, woodsy, like it would if trees grew in the house.

She didn't know them all that well, growing up. Both families were Catholic, but Gloria never saw Hugh at St. Lucy's on Sunday mornings; she found out once they started dating that Livia brought her family over to St. John's on Mulberry Street instead.

Hugh's family lived between her house and the high school, and she'd often fall in behind them as she walked there in the mornings. The four Addonizio boys all looked alike to her. They were stocky, dark, their hair chocolate-colored. They talked lower and yelled louder. To her mind they pushed and shoved more than the Irish boys. That might not have been fair and probably wasn't true.

The Mallons were Black Irish, with blue eyes and light skin and dark hair. Gloria's father, long dead now, had always pointed at her hair and gone on at length about an influx of Spanish blood in the family that dated back to the Armada. Gloria started tuning him out when she was five, and by the time she hit adulthood she'd lost sight of what he'd been talking about.

Hugh had been a grade below her, a year younger and shorter than she was, and she never really noticed him, despite all the times they must have shared space on the sidewalk. She didn't spend any time on boys at all until after high school was over. Her mother Jane may well have run into Livia Addonizio if Jane ever left the house, but she gave no sign of having met any of them before Gloria and Hugh got acquainted at a USO dance downtown in 1940, or at any point after that.

Hugh's father had come over from Naples in 1906 and set up house in New Jersey. Builders, all of them, the whole family, the ones who came to the states and the ones who stayed, but Hugh didn't ever move in that direction. He joined the Army after high school, leaving pudgy and round-faced, coming back a little leaner. Also quieter, more respectful. He was 21, she 22.

They talked a few minutes at the dance about Fordham football — he was a member of the famed Seven Blocks of Granite offensive line, and even she, no football fan, had heard of him — and he sought her ought the day after, knocking at her front door with a bunch of pansies tied with ribbon, but she told her mother to tell him she wasn't feeling well and to come back later. She did the same thing the next time he came by, a few days later, no flowers this time. She watched him walk away and wondered why he didn't try a little harder.

Finally he came back one last time, and she knew if she didn't go down and talk to him he wouldn't come again. She stood on the threshold looking down at him and realized it then: he'd decided on her. His face was set like a quarterback headed into the end zone. He never looked at anybody else again.

Later this week he'd be off for his biannual trip to Puerto Rico with the boys. They went every summer and every winter for a week. No wives, no children, just men on the beach in black socks and sandals, conducting business from the hotel phone. He'd probably ask her to help him pack tonight. Bobby and Jr., ages five and seven, played loudly with metal race cars in the corner of the kitchen, and she had about 20 minutes to get dinner on the table and call them all down before the younger kids got so hungry they started to cry. Gloria stirred the sauce, boiled the spaghetti, turned the kitchen radio on low. She poured a small glass of red wine from the unmarked bottle Hugh's friends always brought Livia when their stock got low.

Marion came down and silently set the table, barefoot in a green cotton shift dress, her Jackie Kennedy bouffant crushed a little on one side where she always held her princess phone. Livia came home, nodding at Gloria as she angled her wide hips through the kitchen door in a faded red and white jacquard dress, its fabric and color much more suitable for curtains. She clutched her brown patent-leather purse and cuddled her black shawl like it was cold out even though it wasn't. It was summer. But still the shawl, pulled so close around her and held so tight she couldn't close the door herself and so didn't try, just left it open and trudged right to her place at the table. Mel Torme sang "Careless Love" on the radio.

Then Hugh came home, stepping through the same door in his suit. He never carried a briefcase and rarely wore a hat, so his hands hung at his sides until they pulled the kitchen door shut. Then he turned toward Gloria and lightly grasped her shoulders. She held her cigarette behind her back as he gave her a small, quick kiss, his face so soft and round she called him her man in the moon. He went right to the table and waited with the children for the food.

Gloria turned around and they were all there. Livia, Marion and Lois sitting quietly, like royalty waiting to be served a feast. The boys still ran around a bit, swatting at each other, waiting to settle until they actually saw the food. Livia had asked Hugh about his day, a string of walk-on appearances at various clubby group headquarters: the Holy Name Society and the Newark American Legion, tomorrow the VFW, the Kiwanis, the Elks. He went from one to another all day and rarely had much to say about any of them.

"Today was a meeting of the Holy Name," he said, settling a cotton napkin on his lap, with an air of ending the conversation the moment he entered it.

"What happens at those meetings, Daddy?" Marion interjected. "I know the group is about preserving the holy names of God and Jesus. But I can't figure out for the life of me what you actually do."

Gloria sat down with the spaghetti and her youngest, Tony, grabbed the bowl. Hugh shrugged.

"Service."

"What kind of service?"

Lois cut in then, as though helping a foreign person learn English: "Service. Food to the hungry. Shelter to the poor. Service."

Marion studied the tablecloth for a moment, then looked up again.

"But do you do the service, Daddy? Do you go to the church and give out the food?"

He studied her.

"Sometimes."

She looked back down at the tablecloth.

"He's the mayor," Livia cut in. "He does all that. He's the mayor. Eat your dinner."

The radio smoothed out into Frank Sinatra's "You Brought a New Kind of Love to Me." Gloria waited for the food to come back to her and looked around the dining room while Frank sang about being a slave to his queen, he'd "work and slave the whole day through if I could hurry home to you," and then the lyrics gave way to the bridge, to waves of strings and drums and horns. Gloria closed her eyes and saw couples twirling together over those blue waves, their azure floor-length skirts flying through the air as they spun, flipping up almost to touch their elegantly outstretched arms.

Then a child said her name and she opened her eyes. One of the boys' socks collected dust under the table, next to a well-loved stuffed dog missing two legs. When her own mother was alive, Jane would have called the place unkempt. The mess rattled Gloria, but she felt powerless against it. She couldn't do anything more about the dust and dirty clothes around this house than she could stop the rain.

Back when Hugh was a Congressman, 1948-62, back when they lived in D.C., there had been Corinne, a lovely light-skinned, older black woman who'd cleaned for Washington families since the stone age. With Corinne, you wore something and left it in a little pile on the closet floor, and you never saw it again until she brought it back, pressed and ready for the next function. Oh, Gloria missed Corrine.

Same with the baby — back in the 50s it was just Marion, and she was just a tiny thing — you just rolled up her diaper and Corinne would slip in silently and spirit it away. Gloria never even had to think about it. Sometimes Hugh would come home and Gloria would still be upstairs, curlers in her hair, flitting about getting ready for some Congressmen's event or other; never mind. Corinne would greet him, take his hat, tell him about their day, giving Gloria another lovely few minutes to finish putting on makeup or brushing her hair, like a lady of leisure. Now they were home in New Jersey, it was 1964, and suddenly somehow there were six children and no Corinne. Gloria had asked around as they'd planned the move from Washington to the big new house in New Shrewsbury, New Jersey, but she hadn't been able to find anybody to help.

Now there were six of them. Six sets of mittens on the floor of the hallway in the winter, covered with snow and dirt, six sets of boots passed down from one to the other until the smallest ones seemed as though a puff of air would blow them apart, their leather edges curling over tiny, dirty socks bared to the elements at the toes every day. Six bags crammed with schoolbooks on the dining room table, canvas binders wet at the edges peeking out and shoved repeatedly back in, the remains of lunch in greasy brown paper tumbling out onto the floor. Six bundles of messes, dirt, dander, leaves and grass in the house all summer and at least one case of lice every fall. Combs and brushes, things that came from animals themselves, never ever clean.

Gloria sipped her wine and saw the homes of her past in her mind. Her parents' tiny tenement apartment in the Central Ward; the Washington apartment she had with Hugh, a dark walk-up with a galley kitchen and pernicious mouse problem. The walls were painted grey-brown and the bathroom was the size of a postage stamp, but Corinne had kept it all clean. Compare it to this New Shrewsbury colonial, with its white walls and wide windows, nine-foot ceilings and rooms big enough for the dust to pile up in the corners, and a kitchen so large the boys could play with toy cars in it at the exact same time Gloria cooked dinner. Because Gloria had to cook dinner now that there was no Corinne.

Another thing about Corinne: she never acted like she wanted to be friends with Gloria necessarily; the two women never looked to each other for advice or help. Corinne was simply a professional who did her job beautifully. She rarely even spoke, really. She didn't need to. She had a warm, wan smile that said everything for her.

After Corinne, in the three years since their move to the Jersey suburbs, there had been Agnes and Olivia, colored women sent up from the city, one in the summer of '63, one in the frozen January of '64, both very different in age and size, both aggressively silent. Gloria intuited that each one hated not only her but the whole family, and after a few weeks they'd just stopped showing up.

* * *

The next morning, Hugh gone downtown, the kids at school and her mother-in-law safely behind her closed bedroom door, Gloria clutched a cup of coffee, turned on the radio and thought she might just have time for a shower when the phone rang. It was Hugh's friend Tony's wife, Marie.

"Honey, we're going to get our hair done Thursday. You should come."

Gloria held onto the phone, so different from her daughter's powder blue princess phone upstairs; the family's main phone was a blocky beige plastic that felt heavy in her hand. She looked out the window and watched a tiny goldfinch hop around on the feeder.

"I don't think Thursday will work," she said in a quiet voice.

Marie cut right to the point.

"When was the last time you left the house, honey?"

Gloria shrugged, forgot Marie couldn't see her. She'd gone to the grocery store yesterday. She went to the grocery store all the time.

"We are picking you up Thursday morning at 10 and we're going to Betty's to get our hair done. This needs to happen. It is time."

"I…there's no time, Marie. There's no time."

"You still don't have help, do you, Gloria?"

Gloria sighed, started to answer, but Marie cut her off.

"I'll tell you what else it's time for. I'm going to have Tony ask the guys. We'll get you somebody good. Somebody Italian. Somebody who knows what they're doing."

"Oh, don't do that, Marie," Gloria sighed. "They're going on that trip. They don't have time for this."

"Yeah, well, I'm going to do something about this situation, Gloria. Just wait. I don't want to bother them on the trip, but if I have to, I have to."

Gloria sat at the table with her coffee, staring out the window. So often during those early years it was just sitting like this, with baby Marion in her lap with a bottle, then a little later baby Lois, watching Marion play on the floor. Gloria and Corinne had warmed bottles and washed diapers. It was so much work, yet it all went so fast. Once she set the boys down off her lap to crawl across the floor, they started instead to run, to the woods behind the house, in the street darting in front of cars, or to J.J. Newberry's, the 5-and-10 cent store downtown. One second she was in the rocker feeding Marion with a bottle, the next Marion disappeared into her parents' bathroom with the princess phone in the big house in New Shrewsbury.

That's where Marion had been this morning, Hugh maneuvering around her to get ready to go. She'd been a total mess, up until all hours on the phone the night before, curlers in her hair and cream on her face, and when she woke up in the morning for school it had smeared on the pillows and her hair came out of the curlers all messy and funny-looking. If he didn't get into and out of that bathroom well before her, she'd careen in there like she was on the run from a bomb. Then she'd lock herself in until ten minutes after she was supposed to have been somewhere else, and if you said anything to her she'd snarl back like a trapped cat.

Gloria had stood at the locked bathroom door today, her own face covered in green cream. She knocked softly, cooing, like trying to get a wild animal into a cage. Four bathrooms in the big new house, but Marion had taken up residence in theirs.

"Honey, can you hear me? Daddy needs to take a shower," she sang.

"I need to take a shower too! Daddy's not the only one who lives here!" Marion shot back, her voice pinging behind the door like change thrown on the ground.

Hugh stood in the hallway, holding a towel, staring at the ceiling. He threw up his hands and got dressed and just left.

"Gloria! Are you still there? Wake up, honey!" Marie yelled through the phone, snapping her back to life.

"All right, then. Ricky's on Thursday, then. Thank you for calling," Gloria said, and hung up.

2

Donnie Agostino had been the mayor's chief of staff about a month. He stood just behind and a little to the right as his boss, Newark Mayor Hugh Addonizio, waited for a crowd to form on the street in front of the brand-new Clinton Hill Apartments, the sun too bright at nine a.m. Everyone — the crowd of four people that Donnie hoped fervently would grow to more — took a minute to line up on the sidewalk in front of the big new building, its gleaming glass doors throwing glare back onto the crowd. The people stood just in front of Hugh and Donnie, so close the mayor didn't really need a podium or even a mic. They were just reporters watching the mayor do what he did all the time at City Hall; today they just happened to be outside.

They were there to open the Clinton Hill Apartments, officially, in that way that involves speeches, red ribbons and big fake scissors. The big development had just been finished, still a little painting to be done inside, its white, modern towers reaching up into the sky, hundreds of feet above the apartments next door. Donnie lived in one of those smaller places, down the street, two-story beige with a stoop and an iron railing to help you up the steps when you came home at night. Nothing like that here. You had to hold yourself up and pull open the glass-and-steel doors of the new Clinton Hill Apartments, like you were walking into a big department store.

Donnie was taller than most people, so lanky he sometimes made others around him look adolescent, unformed. His new shirt was too tight. His girlfriend Clara had picked it out with him just the previous weekend, but the collar scratched his neck, trapping the morning's hot air in there. He stood next to a tree and smelled its dirt and leaves, his back to the new building, the heat wafting up from the sidewalk, shimmering on the city street.

He was nervous, waiting for a crowd to gather. It usually happened when a group of white city men held a press conference on the street in the mixed-race neighborhood. People would naturally drift over to see what was going on. No one seemed in a hurry today. A few people walked languidly by, obviously moving toward work or the store, as Donnie's group got set up. A young colored woman in a robin's-egg blue cotton dress stepped off the sidewalk to avoid them, her shiny shoes clicking to the curb as she stared up at the big new building, annoyed at the intrusion on her way to work. A light breeze stirred some garbage on the sidewalk, moved some paper facedown into a puddle from last night's rain, summer in the city.

They called this neighborhood the Silk Stocking District. It was home to some of the city's most elegant townhouses, some red brick and some pastel, some pearly, gleaming in the sunshine like the jewels they were. Donnie's more modest apartment sat tidily in a two-story brick box about a five-minute walk away. Today the neighborhood smelled of the dirt that crunched under people's feet as they made their way around this motley city group to wherever it was they were supposed to be.

Just then Donnie noticed a group of colored people — it looked like a family; man, woman, grandmother and two adolescent children — standing on the corner just beyond reach of Hugh's voice. They were watching things get ready but keeping their distance. Maybe they'd ventured out for a walk, noticed the tiny crowd gathering on the street and stopped for a look, but didn't want to come any closer.

But Donnie needed them there. He needed to bring the mayor a larger audience. He moved toward them before he thought twice about it, his new shoes scraping the sidewalk, giving off the same purposeful sound as on the City Hall floors. In a sense this errand was no different from the ones at work. He saw something he the mayor needed down the way, and he went to get it for him.

The family eyed him as he came up. Donnie nodded and was about to introduce himself, then realized they knew who he was. A city man, part of the mayor's office. He felt that pride as a palpable wave that started at his feet and rose up the length of his body as he strode toward them. The man didn't meet his eyes, just looked back over Donnie's shoulder to the new building. Donnie focused on him, and the two women and the children actually looked away and stepped to the side, refusing to engage.

Everyone was equal to Donnie, who'd grown up in the Central Ward with Irish, Jewish and Negro children, played in the streets with them right alongside his seemingly hundreds of Italian cousins. But the colored population in Newark had ballooned in his lifetime, so many moving up from the South that the streets overflowed with them now. They'd moved right in alongside the Irish and the Italians and the Jews, many of whom — including the mayor Donnie had just gone to work for — had responded by packing up their own families and fleeing for the suburbs. The newcomers scoured the city for work during the day and packed into big brick towers at night, claiming this whole overcrowded, concrete place for their own.

"What is that place?" the man asked, nodding toward the new building.

"New public housing. It's for families like yours," he said, looking evenly at the man, trying to size up the situation. The man was presentable enough in green cotton shirtsleeves and pants. His shoes were only slightly scuffed. His hands were in his pockets. Why was the whole family out walking around on a weekday morning? Shouldn't the man, at least, have been at work?

If Donnie smiled, he'd seem like he was pandering. If he didn't, they might think he was some menacing government official who hated them. He wanted to point down the street to his own apartment, to show outright that they were all in it together, and he started to open his arms expansively as if to say this was his neighborhood too, this collection of motley buildings close to the street, most low and homey with stoops just steps from work that you could drink your coffee on in the morning. But that felt like too much, somehow, and Donnie let his hands fall to his sides and stay there. No way of knowing where these people lived now, if they had a home or a stoop or a way to pay for any of that. He looked back and sized them all up a bit more, and now began to think maybe they weren't from around here at all.

And the truth was, the new Clinton Hill Apartments were very different from Donnie's place down the street. He'd toured it with the mayor last week. He'd come away thinking this big new building put up by his fair city could be your home, but you had to know what you were doing there. There was no side table just inside the front door to put your keys and wallet, like at Donnie's. Once in the big front door of this new place you simply comported yourself just as you had out-side, looking down at the hard, shiny floor as you queued up for the elevator with several others who would be sharing this home with you, people you probably didn't know. They could be salesmen or teachers or students, of course, but they could also be junkies or thieves. How could you know, in a place so big? You put your head down, kept to yourself and moved quickly to your destination, just like on the sub-way.

The man just looked back up at him, frowned a bit.

"We just moved. We're supposed to move again?" he said, with the smallest twitch of an eyebrow.

"No…" Donnie grasped for words now, shrugged. "You certainly don't have to move. But it could be an option for you."

Now the man frowned openly. The two women started murmuring to each other and his kids, a boy who couldn't have been more than 10 and a girl who looked to be entering her teens, just stood there looking at the ground.

"I certainly don't have to move? But that's the way it works, right?"

he smiled at Donnie now. "It's public. Public housing. Meaning you put us where you want to put us. You move us in, you don't so much as replace the light bulbs when they burn out, you let the junkies all move in then you say, ho! It's not safe here. Y'all got to move now. That's the way it works. Right?"

Donnie looked around, feeling slightly as though the world was tipping, as if to point out that this was a good neighborhood, safe, full of working people, and who wouldn't want to move there?

But he was flummoxed when he opened his mouth to speak. Such a short time into the job, yet he'd noticed the other day that when he thought of the mayor and his staff, when he stepped into the commanding City Hall building every morning, he thought in terms of we. As though he was one with the city of his birth. But in this moment, the man had him dead to rights.

Donnie hadn't heard this point of view, not since he'd joined the mayor's office or before. And he had no answer — not as Donnie Agostino, new in the mayor's office, trying to rustle up an audience for a press conference; not as the Donnie who'd grown up in Newark, saw high school and college as little more than the delivery system for his current job as second command in the city he loved and now looked forward to getting to every morning; not as the Donnie who so looked forward to a day when all Newark residents had good health care and whole, clean lives.

That was the trouble. He had no answer to the man's question. Why wouldn't people want to move, if they were given a place to be that was so much nicer? Donnie was just trying to get an audience for his boss, and here this man asked him to think in a way he'd never thought before.

In the end, his just shrugged at the man again.

"It's a beautiful building. Lots of families like yours are going to come and love it there. Why don't you step down the street with me and find out about it for yourself?" Then he looked back over his shoulder, back down the street at the mayor, who was looking expectantly at him.

They were just about to start. The reporters brought out pads and pencils and stood ready to take notes. Donnie took a chance that if he simply started back down the street, the family might follow. He was shocked when they did, letting him get a good head start, almost as though they didn't want him to know they were there, then took up their place behind the reporters.

Donnie noticed that Hugh never gestured to the big, new building behind him, never turned to look up at it dramatically and get the reporters to really see the place, the way Donnie thought he might have, had he been mayor. Hugh just stood there, facing straight ahead with his arms by his sides, like the former Fordham football player he was, used to squaring his shoulders, putting his head down and barreling through another mayoral day.

Donnie hadn't known about Hugh back when Hugh played football for Fordham, but as Donnie grew from politically astute Newark high-school student to Seton Hall grad, he'd read the paper and watched with no small amount of awe as this soft-spoken son of Italian immigrants, who grew up in the Central Ward just around the corner from Donnie's family, served 14 years in Congress, then came home to kick Leo Carlin out of the mayor's office in '62.

Hugh had attacked Carlin's do-nothing approach on urban renewal and started building bigger, newer, nicer housing in nearly every corner of the city. Clinton Hill Apartments was just the newest and the nicest. Donnie couldn't understand why there weren't more people here to see it open up to the public. Five reporters were in attendance, but they already looked bored. They watched the mayor realize the crowd probably wasn't going to get any bigger, then clear his throat and begin. He thanked them all for coming.

"Today we present the Clinton Hill Apartments to a neighborhood that has been need of this for so long. We are gathered here to welcome all of you to this state-of-the-art dwelling, built on the site of the former Manischewitz factory, so near our most revered home for worship, the Blessed Sacrament Church, which is just around the corner. The Clinton Hill Apartments is 149 units of public housing made possible by the Newark Housing Authority, built at a cost of $4.3 million dollars."

The mayor pointedly looked around then. Donnie noticed, not for the first time, how halting his boss was when he gave speeches like this, how he tended to fade out a bit at the end of his sentences, as though he'd have really preferred to be sitting down, in his home or office, in a comfortable chair.

"This land, and the building we've built here, were essentially gifts from many generous friends," Hugh went on, almost halting again, as though he expected those friends to show up on the street in front of him at any moment. "In fact, I have so many people to thank for these gifts to the people of Newark that I almost don't know where to begin. It took years of work and the support of both the Newark Housing Authority and the Urban Renewal Administration to help us tear down substandard housing nearby and bring us this marvel, the new pride of the Silk Stocking District."

Donnie felt all that as the mayor said it, the automatic swelling that came with the realization of a dream — even though he'd only been with the mayor's office a month, and hadn't been in on any of the building, much less the fundraising and negotiations. It made him feel like he was late to a party he'd had no hand in setting up. Back when he'd been a boy, this was an all-Jewish neighborhood, the best of the best in businesses and buildings. Now people of all races and religions had a place here. His chest felt full and ready to burst.

"It was not easy," the mayor went on. "The building behind us represents a lot of time and effort. There were…problems. But those are over now."

Donnie took in the stately Clinton Avenue homes near the new building, defiantly standing in the shadow of this white behemoth, still getting enough sun for now on such a bright day. It was so bright, actually, that shouldn't at least some of the windows in those houses have been opened, the woman of the house standing there a second to catch the morning breeze? There was no movement in any of the windows in his sight line. Nobody coming out of the front doors. All of the people were on the street, and not too many of them, even. Not enough.

Then the mayor was ending his too-quick speech. He stiffened, and looked like he wanted to leave. But the reporters had questions.

"Tom Cummings, Evening News," said a big blonde man Donnie already knew so well he didn't need to announce himself. Anyway, he was standing so close to the mayor that Hugh probably could smell his breath. "Could you speak to the reason for the delays?"

It was something Donnie had been meaning to ask about. The mayor actually shrugged as he responded.

"Well, you can imagine," he said slowly. "There are several different agencies working in concert with developers to return to Newark and develop a project of this magnitude. It takes time."

Cummings smirked, still so close Hugh could've reached out and touched him, and Donnie saw him as if for the first time, a big Irish brute who would've looked so much more at home on a football field, clad in a reporter's stock trench coat in what must have been 80-degree heat. The coat was thin and a little threadbare, but still.

"That's the only reason?" Cummings said.

Hugh stared flatly at him, spreading his hands in a gesture that said they were done here. Donnie could feel him looking across the street at his car, a new Plymouth Fury with fishtails the girls in the secretarial pool had ooh'd over during a break in Donnie's job interview, wanting to get in it and get on with the rest of his day.

"Of course," the mayor nodded.

3

Most weekday mornings, Donnie would wake up in the apartment that had been in his family since the 1940s, with Clara there in the bed, though she officially still lived in Maplewood with her parents, and they walked to work together. Today they had toast and coffee, ran combs through their hair and headed out down Clinton Street, Donnie toward City Hall and Clara to her job answering phones for the Chief of Police on Green Street.

People pushed past them headed for desks downtown, the same ones every weekday. Shiny Plymouths sailed in from places like South Orange and Essex, headed to Newark Penn to catch Manhattan trains. For a few minutes they were all on the street together, some young and soft, some creaking and halting, all hardening with every step into what they would eventually be.

Clara's heels clicked on the sidewalk as she and Donnie rounded the corner and headed down Broad Street past Symphony Hall, its incongruous classical columns soaring high up into the hot air. They passed under the marquis advertising the Rolling Stones' upcoming concert, the fourth stop on the scruffy band's second American tour.

She slowed down as they passed the poster, its big type blaring "The World's Hottest Group, Back in the U.S.A. Again!" next to a black-

and-white photo of the long-haired band staring balefully out at pass-ersby.

"I know you like them," Donnie said as she took in the poster as if seeing it for the first time, though they'd walked past it every day for weeks.

"Don't you?" she said evenly.

"Not when I look at this poster," he said, gesturing toward a sullen Keith Richards. "It makes them look like they need a sandwich."

They didn't discuss the Stones, or much of anything else, for the rest of the way to work.

Donnie didn't spend a lot of time with music generally. His parents had died when he was young. When she was 15, his sister Doris had taken over the apartment in Clinton Hill and the duty to bring up Donnie until she married and moved to Plainfield with her husband four years later. They studied, they cooked dinner, they watched TV. Doris walked her little brother to baseball practice after school. They rarely thought to listen to music.

Now if he came home from work in the evenings and Clara wasn't there, he'd be more likely to put on the radio and catch some news, or a bit of a ball game. But she liked the Stones quite a bit. She'd played "The Last Time" for him on the hi-fi the week before. Though she stayed over at Donnie's more often than not, she wasn't in the habit of leaving her things around; she'd come and go with smartly packed overnight bags, round and bright with plastic handles that she'd set on the chair in the living room when she arrived, then clicked shut and hefted off when it was time to go. When she came into the apartment, she and her wide musical tastes simply commandeered the place the moment she walked through the door. Sometimes Sinatra, sometimes the Stones, sometimes the same rolling blues and jazz and shouting horns and swinging lyrics he'd catch coming out of colored families' apartments as the two of them walked around the neighborhood after dinner some nights. She loved it all, and he hardly registered any of it. To his mind, there just wasn't time.

Work in the mayor's office was all-encompassing. Donnie ran

through the days, talking to citizens or working at his desk from the moment he walked in the door until some other senior staffer told him it was time to go home. From the time he was a kid he knew he wanted to work for this city, to help its people, his intentions so pure he didn't often bother to tell people about them; he was afraid they'd think he was simple-minded, or else that he had some ulterior motive. There were plenty of guys walking around downtown who would look right in your face and tell you they were just out to help their fellow man. They had one hand behind their backs that filled up with money.

Maybe that's why Donnie wasn't taking to the Rolling Stones. Those boys had to be eating better than anybody, what with the screaming hoards of teenagers waiting to throw their money at show tickets every time the band condescended to come to America. The Stones were probably in their early 20s, younger even than he and Clara, and God knew they couldn't be working all that hard, yet they probably did very well for themselves.

But Donnie had grown up in the Central Ward of Newark, whose population had been 30 percent black since before he was born and never anything but achingly poor. When his mother had been around, she'd set up in the kitchen and cooked ziti twice a week for as many neighbors as she could, delivered by Donnie and Doris to nearby buildings with doors that wouldn't close and broken glass all over the stairwells. But she was gone now, and he knew black families who'd lived down the street for three generations yet still couldn't get doctors or decent jobs.

This week, Donnie been able to help exactly one man, James Cash, by giving him a job in the mayor's office as a clerk. That felt good; it felt solid. James was a slight black man about Donnie's age who was so short that when Donnie looked across his desk and offered him a job to start the following Monday, and then the two stood up to shake hands, the top of James' head came up the the middle of Donnie's chest. But Donnie was tall. He was used to that.

"We hired a man named Cash," Donnie told Clara at home that night as they ate a meager dinner in the kitchen. "Unfortunately he's only the third Negro hire the city has made in probably the last decade. He seems like a good man."

By now Clara had spent two years watching any number of men and women walk into the police station to interview for positions like hers. They'd be hired if they were white and turned away if they weren't. Word had gotten around and nobody who wasn't white even bothered to keep trying. Chief of Police Dominic Santoro never pretended to hold his department to the same standards as the city office.

"It's kind of disgusting," she said around a mouthful of bread. "I go in to my job, I sit down, I'm surrounded by people who look like me. Who are dressed like me. White people. Then I go outside to get a sandwich at lunch, and there are colored people and white people walking around together. I get a sense of what they call the melting pot, is what I'm saying. And then I finish my sandwich, I go back inside, and it's all white again."

Clara sometimes went on about work at dinner, saying she felt so bottled up during the day that she just had to. The fact that to her employers, blacks really had no place except the back of a squad car: nobody ever talked about it, she said.

Donnie didn't mention it at dinner, but he'd heard his own employers talk about it plenty. Just last week, he'd walked shoulder-to-shoulder with his boss down the long, yellow-carpeted pathway at Seton Hall, part of a throng of important people headed to a benefit for somebody he knew nothing about, all the men whispering while they walked, their voices bouncing off the paintings of founders hung on the beige walls. Suddenly Santoro, a dark Italian with a big mustache and a belly like a fat tick, came at Hugh and Donnie from a perpendicular, similarly carpeted hallway. Santoro clapped Hugh on the back and fell in step with him, pushing Donnie back to following both of them. The police chief then started stage-whispering vague insults about a black man his boys had picked up that afternoon outside a bar on Bergen Street. Donnie knew while he listened that he'd never tell Clara what he'd heard. It might make her so angry she'd want to quit, and then where would she be?

So Donnie told Clara he'd hired James Cash, and she reminded him about the public health bill that would go into effect in the fall, and the two of them murmured over linguini that maybe things were actually improving in the city despite people like Santoro. Then they moved to other, more overtly positive topics.

When Donnie got into the office that Monday morning, James was already there, giving off an air of having been hanging around for hours, waiting to get to work. He was standing among the secretaries talking to the mountainous Emelda Ryals, the single colored woman in a ten-secretary pool. Emelda did her job politely and silently, and she wasn't saying why or how she'd held her it for so many years or who'd let her have it in the first place, black or white. Or anyway she might have told James, but she wasn't telling Donnie.

Donnie always put his files and papers and pens away when he left the city office at night, but now there was a brown manilla folder on his desk, right on top of the calendar blotter. There was no writing on the outside of the folder. Donnie sat, set his bag lunch on the desk, and flipped the folder open quickly with one finger, just to see what it was, when James walked up and greeted him.

"I didn't get to meet the mayor when I came in the other day, and now it looks like I won't for awhile," James began, standing in front of Donnie's desk.

Donnie looked back over his shoulder and realized the heavy wooden doors of the mayor's office were closed, and no light came from under them.

"Oh," he said, flustered. "Is he out?"

"Apparently he's way out. Mrs. Ryals says Puerto Rico. For a week."

Because James was watching, Donnie nodded silently, put his hands together on his desk, his way of slowing things down a bit so he could figure how to respond without necessarily telling James he hadn't known the mayor's schedule this week. Of course James, still dressed in a shiny green suit jacket because no one had yet told him he could take it off and put it down on the back of a chair, didn't care whether Donnie had known or not. James had been on the job thirty minutes.

He didn't know yet where he was supposed to sit.

Donnie mentally scheduled the tour of the office he was expected to give his new hire in the next few minutes, his eyes landing back on the brown folder. He felt James watch him as he scanned the contents. There was one sheet of loose-leaf note paper with about a dozen handwritten numbers with dashes, like social security numbers, except there were no names attached. There was no text on the sheet at all, just the numbers. Nothing he could give James or anybody else to work on, since Donnie had no idea who'd left it on his desk in the first place, or what he was supposed to do with it. He could take it across the hall to one of the mayor's senior people, clerks and lawyers and longtime secretaries — the ones who had helped Donnie over the last weeks and months to really figure out what he was supposed to be doing — but not for a few minutes, until James was safely squared away.

In the end Donnie brought James to Anita McHaley, Hugh's secretary, a nice Italian girl from the neighborhood who'd married an Irish cop from two blocks away, both families living so close to the Agostinos that the members of all three families could probably have heard one another snore at night, had they tried.

Anita asked if Donnie wanted to call Hugh.

"In Puerto Rico?" Donnie said. "He has an office in Puerto Rico?"

"No, but he stays at the same hotel whenever he goes down there. They know him, and if we have to sometimes we can call. We try not to, though."

Donnie wanted to ask why the mayor wouldn't have let him know why he was going on vacation, but James was still standing there. So he more or less shoved James at Anita, murmuring something about how they might want to look into any necessary mayoral rescheduling.

Then he darted across the hall to the mayor's senior staff member Frank Addonizio, no relation. Frank was nearly as tall as Donnie, as Donnie would know if he'd ever seen the older man anywhere but leaning way back in a squeaky wooden chair behind a huge oak desk, piled with paperwork.

"Do you know what this is?" Donnie said, by way of hello, holding the folder up in front of him. He took the piece of paper out and held it aloft, so that Frank could see what it was: just a list of numbers.

Frank furrowed huge, unkempt brows, the effort making his long-ish grey hair bob over his forehead for a second.

"Do I know what what is?"

"It was on my desk. Just a bunch of numbers."

Frank leaned forward. He rarely did that.

"Those were on your desk?"

Donnie raised his own brows in answer, let the hand with the folder rest down by his side.

"If they were on your desk," Frank said, "you must be supposed to deal with them, I would imagine."

Donnie waited, but no more information came. He didn't want to tell Frank he was at sea about what to do.

"Deal with them how, do you know?"

Frank nodded. Apparently he did know.

"You need to take those numbers and enter them into the list of people licensed to contract with the city."

Donnie waited again for more information, but no more information came, so he ventured: "But there are no people's names listed here. How do I know the names for these numbers?"

Frank waved the problem away.

"You don't need to know the names. You just need to know the numbers."

Donnie stared blankly at Frank, who he'd come to think of as deserving of the name. You could just ask him things point-blank, things you had to pussyfoot around with the mayor and the secretaries. You could be frank.

"That just doesn't make any sense," Donnie finally said.

Frank nodded.

"Leave it with me, son," he said magnanimously. "I'll take care of it. You go do your job."

Donnie handed Frank the folder and tried to chalk it up to being new, just another of those tasks he'd understand later, after he'd worked for the city as long as Frank and Emelda Ryals had. Then he went back to sit at his clean desk.

4

James Cash lived at the Hayes Homes, 15C. His lived there with his mother Inez and his brother Fred, who was two years younger than James. Their apartment was spare and quiet, clean but understocked with food and things to do. Rats ran down the long hallways of the huge high-rise, and most of the windows were broken. They called it Brick City, 16 floors of poor people piled on top of each other, towering above the police precinct, which was right across the street and tiny by comparison.

James' girl Lena, at 25 four years older and more together than he ever thought he'd be, lived with her parents in 12D. James' family didn't believe in air conditioning, but Lena's parents kept their unit cranking all day and night, watching the combo HiFi/TV console the Cash family didn't have at their apartment. James and Lena had been together for 18 months. Being with her made him feel pulled a couple notches up in the world.

Lena worked with her mother in an insurance office on Springfield Avenue. That alone was important. It taught him something tangible, how she got up every day, rode an elevator full of dirty needles down to the street and walked around the corner to talk paperwork with white people. She was tall, with soft chocolate-brown skin and hair she rolled most nights in foam curlers. And she calmed him down. She stopped him from stepping into trouble with the gangs of marauding teenagers who trolled the Hayes Homes hallways, hitting up law-abiding citizens and sidestepping the National Housing Authority guards who patrolled the place.

Just last month he and Lena had been leaving her apartment together, headed for the elevator, and he'd heard them coming, laughing and yelling as they rounded the corner, probably on their way to take some old lady's change for the coin laundry. His whole body had tensed. His own mother was just three floors up. She was behind a locked apartment door, but what if she went into the hallway for something? He wanted to jump right in the middle of the pack of kids and start kicking and punching, breaking ribs and poking eyes out. But Lena laid a hand on his arm, said nothing, and he decided that Inez probably wouldn't go out that night, that she was safe upstairs. And then, for the moment, the gang was gone.

Now, finally, James had his own job. A good one, for the city, in the mayor's office, part of an apprenticeship program nobody could tell him the name of, started up after the CORE — the Congress of Racial Equality — business at White Castle last year. Which James hadn't even been involved in until Fred brought it up at dinner one Sunday a year ago, just as things were starting to get going for the loosely arranged, quickly growing cadre of young volunteers bent on making life in the city better for blacks.

Fred had been just 17 then, but built like a fighter, and he'd only found CORE a few months before. But he'd already met Robert Walker, its unflappable leader. He'd already picketed at least one White Castle diner downtown, and more out in the all-white suburb of Orange. Fred drew placards saying "We Want Black and White Castle" and "Bigotry in Business Equals Bankruptcy," then got into cars with bunches of other young men and stopped at every White Castle restaurant they could find for 50 miles. Sometimes other blacks would cross their picket lines. Fred and his friends would yell, "Negro, you're not ready for freedom yet."

It was making Inez crazy. On the first night Fred was headed out to White Castle in Passaic, she plopped pork chops down on the table and then sat down heavily herself, so small and slight she nearly slid off the plastic chair.

"So. The White Castle," she began, out of breath.

Fred already had the plate with the chops in his hands, and he didn't look up as he grasped one in his fingers and laid it on his own dish. He said, "Yes. The White Castle," into his plate of food.

"What do you do there?" Inez was starting off all innocent, wanting to make Fred explain the whole thing.

Fred sighed.

"You know what we do, Mama. I told you. We picket them. We tell them they need to hire more black workers, and serve more black customers. You know. I told you."

Inez shook her head like she didn't understand.

"I heard they threw firecrackers at you. And they took young people to jail."

Fred set his pork chop down.

"No. That was in Brooklyn. They didn't do that in New Jersey. That's in Brooklyn or the Bronx, but not here. It's quieter here."

Inez was silent for a second. Then she said, "Well, I don't see what difference that makes. So it wasn't you they threw fire at this time. It might be you they throw it at next time. That's all."

James was picking at his own chop and only barely registering their conversation. He'd been so into Lena lately he had almost fogotten Fred had been picketing White Castles.

All three of them registered this fact in the same moment. Then Inez and Fred watched him try to catch up with them.

"I thought we had some jobs at White Castles," James started out.

"No," Fred said, in the plaintive way he had. "We have four. Four jobs out of 126 in New Jersey. And they don't want us eating there. So this is a good move."

James looked at Inez as though that explained things, and Inez looked back at James like he had two heads.

She looked down at her plate, pointed at her older son with her fork.

"You go with him," was all she said.

So now it was James' job to shadow Fred whenever he went to CORE meetings, whenever Inez thought he might be getting ready to go yell at people across picket lines. The first time James showed up at White Castle, he met the moon-faced Bob Walker, who told him where he was really needed: at construction sites. That was White Castle times a hundred, Walker said.

Walker wore a sports jacket and had a nice watch. He was poised and self-assured. And he told James that if he really wanted to help, he'd go down to where they were building Barringer High School downtown; he'd go down to where they were building Rutgers University's new law school. They'd promised to hire Negros and Puerto Ricans, lots of them. And no Negros or Puerto Ricans had ever been hired.

They were lying, Walker said, but it wasn't like you could tell them you knew that. You had to go down there, ask questions, be polite. You had to point things out in a civilized way. Only then would the city men ever take notice.

"We go down there waving signs and yelling," Walker said, his hands on his knees in a booth in the South Orange White Castle, "we figure, that's not working anymore. So you go down there, young man. Go down there and be nice."

So James went down there the following week, no Fred or placards in tow, just to check things out. He met Mayor Hugh Addonizio and his chief of staff, Donnie. He was polite to them. He asked questions. They were polite to him. James knew the mayor had recently bought a new five-bedroom colonial in New Shrewsbury, the very thought of which made Brick City feel like a dank prison. Standing beside him and chatting, James felt like an inmate out on good behavior. But what the three men actually said to one another was all very civilized.

And just like that, James ingratiated himself with the city men. He only had to show up at a few more construction sites before Walker crowned him the cool-headed mouthpiece for the militants — James, who'd knocked around in this or that job since high school, trying to figure out what it was he really wanted to do. James, who didn't have much of a head for money or politics, but who definitely saw himself as a husband and father someday, and thought those things would probably line themselves up pretty nicely if people would just let him spend a little more time with his girlfriend.

After awhile Fred seemed to cool it on the White Castles, or if he still actively picketed them, he didn't tell the family much about it anymore. James got back into looking for work and spending as much time as possible with Lena. Then Fred must have told somebody at CORE that James was looking for a job. Or something. Because Donnie from the mayor's office called Inez at the apartment and offered James a job. Inez accepted for him on the spot.

So he made his way out Monday morning, clanging and bumping down 15 dark flights on the elevator. A couple teenaged girls got on at the eighth floor. One had dirty white sandals not hitched at the heel, the white peeling away after dragging on the dirty Brick City floors. The other wore navy sneakers with white trim and holes at the toes. They stood over in the corner together, smiling and whispering behind their hands, sneaking looks at him and then pretending to stare down at their feet. James wore a shiny suit for his new job, and he forgot for a minute that he was only a few years older than they were. He stared straight ahead at the elevator doors and felt admired. The three of them rode from 8 down to the bottom, staring at the two pairs of shoes in the dark elevator corner. Then the doors opened and the girls shot out as if on an urgent errand.

Though when he'd gone into the office today for the first time, nobody could really tell him what to do. The mayor was out of town and Donnie had been no help. But no matter. He was on the payroll now. He'd figure it out.

5

Sometimes Tony Boy Boiardo felt like he could only really tell what the hell was happening in New Jersey from the vantage point of a plastic chair in Puerto Rico.

He spent too much time lately driving from meeting to meeting, each one less fun than the one before. And when you worked for family, as he had for his father since before he was tall enough to see over the kitchen countertop, you were never off duty, not unless you got up and left the country. The little junkets with Hugh and Big Marty and maybe a couple of other key guys you were working with, traveling to an intimate island on a tiny plane with a bunch of little vodka bottles balanced on the seatback tray — that's how you kept everything straight.

The Americana hotel was a was a four-story, grey cinderblock place that looked like it had been dropped from space to sit on the sand, flocked by a few man-sized palms. Tony checked in alone on Tuesday afternoon, saying as few words as humanly possible to Juan at the front desk before scurrying to his room. Big Marty and Hugh would come sometime later, separately.

Usually Tony would change into a guayabera and plastic sandals, spend a few minutes on the tiny patio outside his room on on a thin metal chair, then meet the guys back at the bar. This time he left the light, party-ready shirt in the suitcase, just stripped down to his t-shirt and a pair of Bermudas, left his socks on. Propped open the sliding glass door and hit that metal chair like it was his bed after a long trip, looked out at the waves and tried to think of nothing.

He felt like he never really calmed down, not even here. In fact, all these trips tended to have the same rhythm: the tension coming off the men in attendance started off low in the morning and thrummed like a rubber band as the day got longer, so that by the time they sat behind the first a couple of drinks in the early afternoon, they were all jumping out of their skin, needing heavy medicine to smooth out all the kinks in their heads.

Tonight they sat with their backs to the water, watching dark-haired waiters in white cotton shirts run drinks with pink umbrellas through the sand. A group of local girls hung out in the lobby bar, dressed for the pool, sneaking smiles at all the men, even the ones out with their wives. This place gave you a boy for your whole stay to run cocktails and messages and pretend they didn't speak any English when people called — but if it was urgent, a waiter would bring a phone with a 100-foot cord, leave at the table for as long as you needed it, and disappear.

As the sun went down, they talked about building things. The Italians have always been builders. Hugh, Tony, Big Marty, they built things together. Big new buildings that took years and gave guys jobs and transformed the way Newark looked and its people lived. It was just that they had to go through so much to get things done. Everything took forever because nothing happened without elaborately set-up, tense meetings with Tony's father, Richie, who ran everything from his mansion in Livingston. They met there, in the ornate stone palace that still filled Tony with dread, even though he'd grown up pedaling his trike down its marble halls.

Hugh didn't have to go see Richie much. Big Marty did, though when he did go he was mostly silent. You couldn't really get inside the guy's head, but Tony Boy was pretty sure Marty didn't like the situation much either.

Marty always cut an impressive figure on the job. Tony admired it. Marty would start with a solid shirt, short-sleeved, businessman-style — in, say, cornflower blue. He'd pair it with a darker pant, like a royal blue. Then over that a blazer, plaid, that picked up those dominant colors and wove them through with others. In the winter, big sweaters in XXL that matched his trousers, because Marty was tall, and not slim. His wife Lila helped him pick everything out. He looked good. But tonight he just seemed out of it.

They'd developed a pattern over the years. Most of the business happened at night, in as few words as possible, at a small table between the beach and the bar, Hugh and Tony and usually Richie or Big Marty drinking scotch over melting cubes slowly but steadily, starting at about four in the afternoon. They'd talk about things that were in motion, things that had to be done now, small details that would blow everything up if you didn't tend to them. Only rarely were the really big ideas discussed at dinner; big ideas were for long plane rides, for staring at the sea in your metal chair outside your room.

"I don't know what it is," Marty was saying, seemingly to himself, as they nursed their first drinks. "Back home I wear layers like they say to but I can never get warm. Here I got nothin' on practically all day, it's no problem."

Hugh and Tony just looked at him for a moment, Marty's words not sinking all the way in, as though he was speaking Chinese.

"But it's summer," Tony finally said.

"I know it's summer now," Marty stammered. "I'm talking about when it's winter."

The evening was just beginning, and already Tony felt like he couldn't hold his head up anymore. He plunked his elbows down on the table and rested his forehead in his hands.

"How are we supposed to know that?" he mumbled at Marty, staring down at the table. He'd known this man since childhood, but for some reason looking at him tonight wound him up into knots.

Hugh said nothing. He just looked over the water and pretended nobody was talking.

Tony felt peevish, and tried again with Marty.

"Well…ok," he said, making the effort to sit up now and make eye contact with his friend. "Here, the sand, the sun, your skin, everything's the same temperature," he said. "Maybe that's it."

"Maybe," Marty allowed, but he was grimacing. "But even in the summer, like now, when it's the same temperature there, I'm talking about. Same temperature, down here and up there. I just can't get warm up there, is what I'm saying."

Then Marty dropped the topic, and so did the others. Hugh was still just staring off into space. Then he gestured out to his left, over the water.

"I keep looking out there…but I don't see out there."

Tony waited. Hugh let his hand drop back onto the table.

"Why? What do you see?" Tony finally said. Were they all going to lose their marbles, right here, tonight in Puerto Rico, on vacation?

Hugh looked at him with disappointment. He'd been friends with Hugh for decades; they'd danced at one another's weddings, patted each other's childrens' heads at Sunday ziti dinners, golfed together, all that.

He expects me to know, Tony thought, and I don't, because I can't keep up with this shit. I see you all the fucking time, Tony thought, staring right at Hugh. Why don't I know what you're talking about now?

"He's talking about that plot of land downtown. Where the coloreds live in that big project," Marty said, around a mouthful of shrimp. "It's dark, and dirty. It's unsafe. He wants to tear it down."

Finally something Tony knew how to deal with.

"Well, that's what we do, right?" he said, relieved. "So what's the problem?"

Neither man answered.

Tony set his napkin down and glared at the two of them. He wasn't about to be played like this. A second ago Marty was babbling about the weather, now he and Hugh were keeping secrets. They would damn well tell him what they were talking about.

After a few seconds a kind of wordless pact seem to pass between Hugh and Big Marty. It seemed to Tony that Marty flicked his eyes at Hugh, and Hugh nodded back almost imperceptibly. But he could have imagined the whole thing.

"The medical school needs to get out of Jersey City and Hugh wants to put them in Newark, on that land. But they don't want to go. They don't want to come to Newark."

Hugh shrugged, conciliatory.

"It's upsetting," he said, softly.

"The thing about it is, Hughie's gonna be governor in a couple years, right?" Marty said. "These med school guys, they've got to leave Jersey City anyway, like tomorrow. These guys need Hughie more than he needs them. But right now, they don't know that. They want to be in the suburbs."

Tony waited.

"So," said Marty, recapping, "Hughie goes up to see the trustees, he invites them to come to the city office to see the plans, but they won't confirm. So we'll see. Maybe they'll see reason. But right now they want to go to Madison, somewhere they got a lot of land. So they say they want a lot more land from Hughie if they're gonna go to Newark. They're holding out on us."

"I see," Tony Boy said. Then, to Hugh, he said, "Do you have it? The extra land?"

"I don't know," Hugh said. "I'm trying."

"It's dark, dirty housing projects now," Marty said, finishing up another shrimp. "It could be big, beautiful gleaming buildings, people in white coats going in and out all day. Men of medicine."

Marty picked up his bread again, looked at it as though he might eat it, but put it back down, shrugging.

"Anyway, it would be nice."

As he finished, Marty nodded at Hugh, who nodded back almost sadly, and chimed in: "It would be nice."

They were silent for awhile as they finished their dinner, no one speaking until a pretty waitress came by to refill their drinks. Then

Marty picked things back up.

"I'll tell you one thing, though. My agita. Here, there…. It never goes away," he looked pointedly at Hugh and Tony, inviting them back into conversation. "It's like there's a goddamned little bird in there, fluttering. I get out of breath sometimes."

He said this last with his eyes bugged out. Now he was begging one of them to weigh in.

"You work too hard. You're always working," Tony finally said, shrugging, taking a big swig of scotch.

"Ach, it's true," Marty said, grateful.

Tony saw the opportunity to talk, and took it. It felt like walking out on a tightrope.

"You live with my pop, you work all the time. That's how it is," he started out. "Even now I don't stay up at the house anymore. Even now I got my own place and wife. I'm supposed to be my own man. I'm not," he shook his head and ripped at his own bread, tossed a piece into his mouth and downed his drink, shaking his head. "That's bullshit. I'm not."

They both instinctively looked toward Hugh now, knowing that all this was more talk then he liked to hear. But instead of shutting them down, he shrugged again, made a smoothing motion on the table with his hands; looked right at Tony Boy.

"It's an impossible situation," he said. But he didn't say which situation he was talking about.

Then he was lost in thought again and Tony and Marty saw the phone coming, held backward in the waiter's left hand, the right holding the cord rolled up like a garden hose. The waiter was an older man, so he moved a little slow. Tony was surprised when the phone hit their table, and not someone else's. They weren't expecting any calls. The waiter held the receiver out waiting for one of the men to take it. For a moment they all kept their hands in their laps and looked down at their plates.

Marty seemed to see that he was doing all the talking tonight, so he should get the phone. He picked up the receiver, said hello, and then said okay a few times. Then he hung up and resumed drinking his scotch.

"What was that about?" Hugh asked after a few seconds.

"I'm not sure exactly," he said, leaning way back in his metal chair, stretching his legs out and crossing them at the ankles, folding his hands over his growing gut and looking directly across the table at Hugh. "But apparently we need to help you find a housekeeper."

December 1966

6

There he was at the edge of her bed, whispering "Gloria," because it was still early, most of the kids still asleep. She opened one eye to see he was dressed in a grey suit and tie, on his way to work with his hat in hand, leaning down to jostle her knee a bit to wake her up. She was wrapped up in covers against the cold morning. He was usually out by seven for the hour-long ride to City Hall, and most of the time he didn't bother to wake her.

She sat up, smoothed her hair, reached for her robe. He sat down on the bed, looked right at her.

"I left you some money. Over on the dresser."

She blinked at him, fought back a groggy blip of anxiety. She had plenty of money, cash he gave her every week to keep the house, buy the groceries, things like that. He was looking at her like she should have known what he was talking about.

"You need to buy a new dress," he said. "We've got a special date coming up."

It was as though he'd said relax, it's nothing bad. Now she squinted at him, sitting right there on her bed yet somehow already gone, ready to rush off to his workaday world. His birthday wasn't till after the New Year. Christmas was weeks away; they'd do it like they'd always done it, with meat and pasta and wine and presents, children running around everywhere, quiet and safe at home. Why a new dress?

He read her instantly.

"I'm taking you out to a special function tomorrow night. You'll have fun. But get a dress."

She blinked again.

"When? Where?" she finally said.

He stood up to go.

"It's an event in Hoboken. Everyone will be there. Frank Sinatra will be there. Your favorite singer. You'll want to look nice."

And then he was off to work, leaving her sitting up in bed, still blinking, but starting to plan, a bit of excitement creeping in with the sunshine under the bedroom curtains. Had Hugh noticed how she smiled to herself when Old Blue Eyes came on the radio? He never made her come to other official functions anymore, but he'd been saving this one especially for her. He knew she'd be so excited he'd waited until the morning before, as if she were a kid under the Christmas tree.

Marion could babysit now, especially if Gloria gave her a little of the money on the dresser. Their daughter, 16 now, had just broken things off with her boyfriend and suddenly wanted to be home all the time anyway. She could make dinner for the younger ones, put them to bed, keep things quiet until Hugh and Gloria got home.

Not that Marion could be counted on to help clean up. They'd never found anybody to help with that. Friends had tried back in the summer to find them someone, but nothing ever came of it. Gloria still did most of it herself, every day the cooking and washing and picking up.

Except now she was going out to an event with champagne and tablecloths, and it would be like back when they lived in Washington. Back more than 15 years ago now, when her husband was the freshman Democrat from New Jersey, she the lovely young wife and Marion a pretty baby who already knew how to pose for pictures. Back before their bodies got soft, back when they really talked about things and other people took an interest, invited them places, when their whole lives stretched out before them like miles of perfect turnpike road, back before six children.

These days Gloria almost never went to Newark anymore. She'd stopped going to official functions after Hugh became mayor four years ago; he'd just been re-elected this year and this time she didn't have to do so much as step out to a ladies' luncheon. He just did everything on his own and she stayed home with Livia and the children. She and Hugh only ever got out for dinner occasionally, and then it was often just to Gambardi's in the neighborhood, passable and bland even to her own Irish palate, where people watched them walk in and called out, "Mr. Mayor! How's the family?" and then didn't wait for a response.

And a new dress. Something tony enough for a big event with Frank Sinatra, but warm enough for early December — black or maybe shiny silver with a fitted jacket that she could take off when they got inside and sat down.

She'd worked for Entwhistle's during her teens and 20s, helping other women find the dresses that most became them, standing outside the fitting-room door murmuring encouragements to women she didn't know and nodding knowingly when they stepped out in smart new frocks. She felt effective in her work back then, quietly prideful, learning a trade and bringing money home to her mother.

But she hadn't really bothered to keep track of what women were wearing to events in the last few years. And she was older now. What skirt length was appropriate for a middle-aged mother of six?

She'd have to get a girlfriend to go shopping with her; maybe Lila, Martin's wife. But maybe not. Lila had always been so fun, such a bouncy voice on the phone during their twice-weekly calls. Lately though, Lila seemed sad. She and Gloria talked about it, but only obliquely: Lila never said the words depressed or angry. Gloria had known people who felt that way, might have known what to tell Lila about it. But Lila didn't call it that. Lila said she was downhearted. Downhearted felt so like Gloria's own thoughts lately that the word was like the mirrors on the second floor, the ones she passed so quickly there was no time to register that she was getting older and needed a haircut.

Then there was Marie, Tony's wife. Gloria had known her forever, saw her at least every third Sunday for dinner, but they weren't really close. Marie was brash with a blonde bouffant and wore polyester pantsuits that swished when she walked. Gloria pictured shopping with Marie, trying to focus on finding a dress while Marie loudly denigrated her three children, her husband, her scary, domineering father-in-law. And then she thought about lunching downtown with Marie to more of the same. Sometimes, when she had to shout at the dinner table to be heard above the din of young children, Gloria reminded herself of Marie, and the comparison stung. She would not call Marie.

Ultimately she shopped alone, dropping Hugh at the office, swinging the car through snow flurries downtown while Count Basie's orchestra played on the radio. Then came Sinatra.

She smiled. He really was her favorite. She kept the radio on all the time at home, so it was as if these suave, interesting men — Sinatra, Al Martino, Tony Bennett — stopped in during the day to spend time with her. Now it felt as though Sinatra was there with her in the car, flooding her with pleasant feelings, his "Nice and Easy" starting just as she glided her husband's shiny powder blue Plymouth Fury into the angled space. She'd never driven at all back before the children, but she used the car so much for grocery shopping now that she was practically expert at parking it.

She sat for a moment watching snow fall outside the car, perfect white that never lasted long enough, that would probably be darkened by soot and feet by the time she came out of the store. She was going into Bamberger's department store to shop for a dress. Why was her heart pounding? Because it was exciting to be out, shopping for only herself, planning a night out at an important function with celebrities. "What's your hurry, don't you worry," Sinatra sang. So she sat still for a moment once she'd turned off the ignition, excited, feeling dreamy like she used to, listening until the end of the song. When it came, she reached out to touch the radio knob, but the announcer's voice jumped in the second before she clicked it off.

"Ah, that's a nice one," came a man's smooth, low voice. "That's

Frank Sinatra from a couple of years ago with 'Nice and Easy,' a reminder to take it nice and easy on his special day. That's right, folks; Old Blue Eyes is 51 today. We'll be playing his hits for you today, all day long, right here on WNEW."

Gloria walked into the store and stealthily scouted out dresses on the nearly silent third floor, willing the relaxed, excited feeling to stay with her. She tried on a charcoal-grey embroidered taffeta with rhinestone-studded flower accents on the collar. It was so tight from hips to knees that she had to stand on tiptoes and put one foot in front of the other, back and forth, prancing around in the fitting room in front of the mirror, feeling like a beauty contestant. It smoothed her out in all the right places, but she'd have to sit down slowly, carefully, like a dress model. It was perfect.

"Take it nice and easy — to rush would be a crime," Sinatra had sung to her, back in the car. Her purchase paid for, there was enough left over for a grilled cheese at the store's luncheonette, eaten alone among the businessmen. She looked for her reflection in the shiny pine paneling and reveled in speaking to no one.

Her lunch over, she paid the bill and slowly exited the restaurant, walking down the street to the car as if on eggshells like the dress models did, her purchase in a plastic bag over her arm, proof positive of the important work she'd done here today. Her feet dragged almost imperceptibly as she got up to the car. If only this solitary, purposeful afternoon could last.

She hadn't, in fact, turned the radio off completely. So when she turned on the Fury's ignition, he was there again: Sinatra singing "The Tender Trap." "Those eyes, those sighs, they're part of the tender trap." She pulled out and turned it up, hummed along with the trumpets at the Springfield Avenue light. The song reached its end before the light turned green, Sinatra singing, "you wonder how it all came about … it's too late now, there's no getting out."

Gloria knew the words well. But today, waiting at the light, it felt like hearing a message for the first time. She knit her brow, just a bit, but felt it, realized she'd heard this song 100 times, but never really listened. It wasn't like he was saying he's in love and everything's wonderful. Today the lyrics sounded more like he'd been tricked.

She gripped the wheel, went through two more lights. At light number three, she made her face relax. So what if Sinatra's trapped, she thought. Sinatra's a man. He marries movie stars. Sinatra can do whatever he wants.

"Witchcraft" came on next, its strings like wispy fog. Old Blue Eyes sounded almost somber, singing "there's no nicer witch than you," followed by screaming horns that made her turn the volume down. Frowning again, gripping the wheel, she pulled onto the Jersey Turnpike. Maybe this was why he was her favorite: because it wasn't all wine and roses with him. Maybe it was because sometimes he sang about being stuck in love, about being in trouble, while the other crooners only focused on the good stuff. But today, she wanted a little more of that good stuff. By the time she reached New Shrewsbury, she'd turned the radio off.

She left the new dress in the bag until it was time, then slid silently into it and snuck into Marion's room to have her zip up the back. Her 10 year-old black stilettos went perfectly with the dress. She walked to the landing at the top of the stairs to see him standing at the bottom, looking dapper in his suit to be sure, but he wore suits every day. He looked up and smiled, and she felt like a present waiting to be opened on Christmas morning.

Hugh drove through the rain to Hoboken. He didn't say it, but he seemed excited too. It was snowing lightly, but not sticking, flakes disappearing once they settled on the slick black of the parking lot outside the Legion Hall. Hugh came around to her side of the car to open her door, she fretted that she'd slip in her high heels as she walked across the lot and inside. But each step she took was firm and assured; she needn't have worried.

He walked her into the hall, lit only by candles in the middle of big, round tables. No music, just the low murmur of conversation and cutlery. He pulled out her chair and then, when she sat down, walked around to the other side, to where Martin and Tony sat. Usually when her husband's friends came to the house, they'd see her in her house-dress and come over and greet her first thing, hug her and tell her she looked wonderful. But tonight, now that she knew she really did look wonderful, they didn't. They sat back down and huddled with Hugh, as though they were resuming a meeting.

She'd been sitting at their table for few minutes, feeling so beautiful but so uncomfortable, the chairs on either side of her empty, the champagne glasses in front of each ready. She looked up on the dais and saw Dolly Sinatra, Old Blue Eyes' mother dear. Blonde hair and blue eyes, arms as big as hams in a black lace dress, lifting her glass.

Gloria looked across the huge round table at her husband, seated next to Tony and Martin, the three of them leaning in to whisper-speak with some other big Italian she'd never seen. It took her a second to get him to meet her eyes, and then she mouthed "Is that Dolly Sinatra?" at him. He smiled and gave her a tiny nod.

So where was Frank? Was he somewhere in the audience? Don't look, Gloria. Do not look. Just reach out and pick up your glass. Look at the pretty candle at the center of the table. Don't be an idiot. Don't look around.

And what of Frank Sinatra anyway, she thought, looking for her reflection in the glass, steadily sipping and feeling tipsy instantly, the way she never did at home with wine. What was it about that man that women of every age — even Marion and Lois loved Sinatra, right along with that Vic Dana young person they absolutely idolized, Frank old enough to be ... well, he was their father's age, of course. What was it about him that made them all so gaga? The smooth, dark voice, the tan, the blue eyes, the gruff jokes? Speaking of which, there was no music playing in the room, just the low hum of men talking, the clinking of glasses and silverware, but no singing, no orchestra. But she couldn't see much from where they sat, near the front, facing the stage.

Goodness, she'd been listening to him since Marion was a baby, but when she saw him on TV or in the print ads, he never seemed to age. The thought made her look around for him again, just to see what he might look like now. The radio announcer had said he was in his 50s.

He must have the same crow's feet she did. Was he even here, or had it all been some joke? She would not look around for him. Look into the champagne glass. Scan the crowd for a female friend — she was surrounded by big men in dark suits, no women she recognized anywhere in attendance for some reason, Lila, gone; Marie, gone. Why weren't they with their husbands? Why only her, here in Hoboken surrounded by men?

Gloria's champagne was gone. Was she drunk already? Where was Frank Sinatra? Do not look around for Frank Sinatra.

And then, there he was. On the dais, seated next to his mother, folded up next to her like a package that had just been set there, so much smaller than she was, holding his arms in tight and bent down to listen as she spoke close in to his ear. There were microphones in front of both of them, but they seemed to be off for now; you couldn't hear what she was saying. He was frowning and nodding. He was staring at the tablecloth. Frank Sinatra! Fifteen feet away. Wonders never ceased.

The father, the father must be Italian, because big Dolly Sinatra simply could not be. She had to be Irish, had to be — she was big and round with blonde hair, white as a sheet and broad as a barn, pearls and a crucifix around her neck. She looked like the Pillsbury Dough-boy. But there was no father up there next to Frank and Dolly. They were up there alone, surrounded by empty chairs; presumably people would come up and sit next to them and make speeches or something.

Gloria realized she still didn't know the name of the event she was attending or what everyone around her was supposed to be doing. She would have kept sipping champagne, but it was gone. Not to worry, though, a tuxedoed waiter was heading her way. Drink up, all you people. Order anything you see.

Waiters came around with rare roast beef, mashed potatoes shaped into pretty coronets, more champagne. She'd skipped lunch fearing she wouldn't fit the dress. Now music was coming from somewhere, instrumental, flutes and trumpets but no words, maybe so as not to insult Blue Eyes' sensibility? But then Frank couldn't go around his whole life avoiding other people's voices, right? What must that be like? To be Frank Sinatra?

No one was talking to her; it was as if she'd come to someone else's meeting, and everyone had an agenda but her. Hugh was still talking to Martin and Tony far across the table, so low she didn't know how even they could hear him. Angelo De Carlo, an acquaintance of her husband's whom she'd met briefly years ago, nodded to her over his glass from the next table. He was thin with a Roman nose and suggestive eyebrows, dressed in a white suit with a red cummerbund and a bow tie.

She snuck looks at Dolly Sinatra, still communing privately with her son in the front of the room as she tore into her meat, staring at the fork and knife as tight lips formed words only he could hear.

Then Frank stood up and dinged his fork against his glass, and suddenly it was okay to look at him. You were supposed to look at him. The men stopped in the middle of their sentences, straightened in their chairs and faced the dais, and Gloria held onto her glass, lifting champagne to her lips again and again, if only to have something to do with her hands.

Frank picked up the mic and started to talk in the parlance of the lounge singer, punchy, aimlessly aggressive, ending every line with the word "baby" as though there was a drummer just offstage ready to punctuate his jokes with the "ba dump bump" he was used to, but there wasn't one. The men murmured appreciatively as he spoke; that would have to do.

Gloria stared, swimming, drinking him in, squinting through his opening monologue. His mother sat and finished dinner, looking up at her son over her huge left shoulder, smiling wanly through her round, black glasses at his jokes about Dean Martin's drinking problem ("Dean gave his wife Jeannie a jaguar and it ate her") and Sammy Davis, Jr. ("He came out with a new book last year, called it 'Yes, I Can.' I sent him a wire, told him 'No, you can't'").

Something made Gloria focus on Dolly now. She'd finished eating and had turned around in her chair to face her son. Frank abruptly stopped joking and started to talk about why they had all come tonight. The event was to honor Dolly, who was apparently ward boss here in Hoboken. All the men in the audience stood at that point, faced the dais and applauded Dolly Sinatra. Dolly turned to face them now, beaming, nodding. Gloria did not stand. She felt swimmy, needed both palms on the dinner table now to feel steady.

Frank waited for the applause to stop like a pro, then resumed talking about all the work his mother did with Italian immigrant women, but he didn't say what the work was. Everyone else seemed to know.

"I'm going to turn 50 this year," Frank told the crowd then. "All thanks to her."

He reached down and touched his mother's shoulder then, kissed her on the top of her head.

"Because I was able to stop her from killing me. See, I dropped out of school. She nearly put me six feet under. She always wanted better from me, better, better. I knew if I didn't make it, she'd just make me want to die."

Everyone laughed as though it was the funniest thing they'd ever heard. Gloria felt naive having thought he'd say something nice.

"She's a ward boss. You know what that means? That means you'd better be nice to her or she'll put you under the water."

More laughter, like Frank was doing some comedy bit. But he wasn't saying anything funny. She imagined her Victor, 10 years old now, 40 years into the future, up in front of an audience talking about her that way. How would that feel? You couldn't tell what Dolly was thinking from watching her, but something about the way she held herself made Gloria think of an expression: "iron fist, velvet glove."

"I'd like to sing a song for you now," Frank said, and Gloria looked around for musicians. She finally saw a small group of them on the far side of the dais, as though they were hiding. The musicians stayed silent for the moment but for a lone oboe, played by a thin man in black tails and a bow tie, who stood so they could all hear him.

"This came out on Capitol Records just last year," Frank said, slow and low, then he stopped and listened with them as the lone oboe finished its phrase. "I don't know. Sometimes I think the oboe is the saddest sound in the world."

Then he sang "September of My Years." It seemed to be from the point of a view of a man who was dying, looking back on his life. It was downright mournful. Her head started to throb.

Hugh came around the table and sat next to Gloria, finally. He pushed their dirty plates out of the way and leaned on the table to look into her eyes. He said nothing, just raised his eyebrows as if to say, "isn't this wonderful?"

She felt dizzy, could only manage: "She doesn't look Italian."

Hugh knew what she meant. He nodded.

"She is, though. And Frank's father is Sicilian. But for years he went under the name Marty O'Brien so he could fight in the Irish-only rings. Did you know that?"

She did not know that. How did he know that? How did he know Dolly Sinatra?

She didn't realize she'd spoken aloud, but Hugh said, "well, she's a ward boss here in Hoboken. So of course I'd know her."

Everybody on the dais was taking some sort of break. Apparently her husband did know Frank Sinatra's mother, and quite well too, as the big woman crawled down from the steps toward their table and sat in the empty seat next to Hugh, after embracing him as though they'd been close all their lives. Gloria's mouth popped open in surprise. She slowly closed it, hoping it looked to people watching as though Dolly had greeted her too. Hugh did not introduce his wife. He turned away from her to focus on Dolly.

The two of them leaned away, whispering, facing away from her. She could hear them talking urgently, but couldn't make out what they were saying. She didn't know what to look at anymore, where to put her hands.

Finally she leaned forward to try to meet Dolly's eyes, introduce herself, maybe say something nice about Frank's birthday, how much she'd been enjoying the evening. The older woman stopped speaking in mid-sentence, her mouth stuck in a frozen syllable, and flashed cold ice-blue eyes at her, drew back as if to throw a punch. Hugh looked back over his shoulder at his wife, said nothing, but sent the same message.

Gloria recoiled, the room spinning, her stomach roiling, and sank back into her chair. She took a deep breath, closed her eyes against all the dirty plates and black suits. They were all, day by day, minute by minute, getting so old.

February 1967

7

Everybody in the mayor's office was sold on the spot for the new medical school. It was perfect. Across the street from the Fairmount Houses, right downtown. Perfect.

Donnie realized halfway through the workday that he'd been muttering "perfect" under his breath for two hours. He sat at his desk with architectural drawings spread out so wide he'd had to move his lunchtime sandwich to an adjacent chair.

The drawings showed a brand-new building for the New Jersey School of Medicine and Dentistry with hand-drawn medical students in white lab coats coming and going, and the words, in neat architect's lettering, "Ground Breaking in June 1967."

Nobody outside City Hall realized it yet, but Newark Mayor Hugh Addonizio was gung-ho to build the largest school of medicine and dentistry in the country right in the middle of Newark. When Hugh talked about it, his eyes got round like he was seeing visions. They'd recreate the state's only home for future doctors and dentists and pack them into a big beautiful building that soared up into the sky.

The drawings had come from Bob Burke, a young city planner who worked down the hall. Two weeks ago, Hugh had told Donnie he'd asked Bob to draw something up — he'd gotten tired of having to describe what the new medical school building would look like by just pointing down the street at the intended site and using his hands to indicate the building's size. Hugh said he planned to go down to Trenton for more meetings with Al Lewis and Tommy Manicotta, a couple of statehouse guys, on the topic, and wanted to bring the drawings to use as a sort of calling card. Ten days ago he'd done just that, setting the whole day aside for the meeting, and making sure Donnie was at his side in Trenton.

Donnie looked down now at the drawings, which bore coffee rings from Manicotta's cup. The man hadn't set his coffee down on the edge, either. There was a big stain right over the depiction of the front of the building, a coffee-colored blob on top of the tiny drawing of a med student holding the door open for his lab-coated colleagues. He remembered the moment when the beefy statehouse flunky set the cup down, of thinking Hugh might rise up out of his seat and choke the man to death. But then when Donnie looked at Hugh, sitting in an armchair just to the right of the man's desk, he was calm, his hands folded in his lap, feet crossed at the ankles, looking like a Buddha or something. Totally unruffled at what hit both Donnie and Hugh at the same time: the realization that the statehouse guys didn't want to even hear about Hugh's plans for the medical school, much less support them.

Hugh had filled Donnie in on the way down to Trenton. To Hugh's mind the only real issue would be wrestling the school from the Seton Hall trustees, who'd dumped it on the Archdiocese in Jersey City five years ago and let them run it into the ground. Hugh knew he'd have to pull it away. But he'd told Donnie it would be easily done. Al and Tommy were the first people Hugh had to see, since they'd just finished shoving through the legislation that had rescued the medical school from the Catholics.

"Those guys in Jersey City…they're not our kind of people," Hugh told him. Donnie had just read a newspaper account of the situation, which called the Jersey City officials "brainless thieves who looted the coffers and packed both the faculty and administration with their extensively unqualified associates."

"...then the school's president and dean died within a month of each other, last Christmas, and were not replaced," Hugh continued.

The upshot was that in the last two years the school had racked up $7 million in debt while turning out 160 MDs who didn't know what they were doing.

So Al and Tommy had the state rescue the school for $4 million, and the governor was footing the bill for the whole thing, because doing nothing would've meant shuttering the state's only medical school in the middle of a re-election year.

Hugh's plan was simple: Move the whole thing west across the turnpike to Newark. Erect a beautiful new building downtown on a vacant lot, land he was working to get slated for urban renewal. Clean everything up at the same time.

Donnie had been sure the mayor would leave him out in the hall while he met with Al and Tommy. He usually did. But Hugh seemed to need him nearby all the rest of that day. He never came out and said it, but he had a way of looking down at his right side and to the empty air next to him as if to say, "I need you in that space." So Donnie came into Manicotta's office and sat down next to Hugh, which meant there was no chair near the desk for Al Lewis, who then spent the whole time pacing and staring at the three of them.

Hugh sat perched in a little chair at the edge of Tommy Manicotta's desk like he was asking a banker for a loan. Tommy leaned back in his big leather statehouse chair, fingers folded over his spreading gut, and looked out at Hugh like he wanted to make him feel small.

"Let me get this straight," Tommy said, bellying up to his desk now like he was trying to show he was paying attention, his elbows on the blotter, throwing Donnie a sidelong glance.

"You want the medical school. With the worst reputation in country. In the middle of downtown Newark. Right?"

He wanted Hugh to nod, like a schoolboy, like a patsy. Hugh just stared at him.

"Now you know these are the same guys who they gave 48 hours to get out of Jersey City because of all the bullshit they pulled up there? You know that, right?" Lewis said.

Donnie had never actually heard the details what had happened in Jersey City, why the feds swooped in suddenly one Wednesday night and threatened to close the whole place down by the weekend. But he knew from his own undergraduate work at Seton Hall in public health that a process like that — closing down a school, sending all the professors and students home — normally takes years, not days. It sounded to Donnie like the Jersey City boys were colossal idiots. Hugh said he thought the Archdiocese people were just trying to do the right thing. But who knew?

"You know they wanted Rutgers to take those boys, right? Just give Rutgers the keys to the whole place," Al finally said, like trying to talk reason to a crazy man. "You know what they said over at Rutgers? They said fuck no."

Donnie could tell by the look on Hugh's face that he hadn't exactly known that. Hugh looked back at Tommy and Tommy flexed his hands, glanced down at his desk, shrugged.

They were all quiet for a moment.

"Anyway, these guys don't want to go to Newark," Tommy finally said. "They've got an offer from the Dodge Estate, down the road in Madison. They've got 125 acres. It's nice there. Grassy. Quiet."

Hugh recoiled.

"I heard that's what they wanted, a couple of months ago. But we told them we had 80, and they said they'd consider it."

Tommy just nodded.

"We've got 80 acres for them," Hugh said again. "Now they want more? What happened?"

Tommy nodded again, then shrugged, like it was all out of his hands.

"They're telling us they want to go to Madison," he said. "They did consider it, Mr. Mayor, and they don't want to go to Newark."

For a moment it was silent in the office, then Tommy said, "So if you want this school in Newark, we're going to have to talk."

In the end, things got very quiet. Hugh made his case, Donnie at his right hand, and they said they'd see what they could do.

"You have friends," Hugh said at one point. "We have friends. We can do this. This needs to happen for Newark. We can give them 100 acres."

Tommy said, "But they want 125."

Donnie watched his boss take a shallow breath and hold it in. A few seconds later Hugh said, "We can do it. Come up to Newark next week. We'll show you the plans."

Donnie wanted to whip his head around and stare at his boss now. Freeing up 125 acres on the spot Hugh had in mind would have meant knocking down the Immaculate Heart of Mary church, built in 1822. Where was Hugh thinking he'd put the school?

Hugh wouldn't discuss it on the whole ride back up to Newark. Once they got there, he made a beeline for Bob Burke's office. When Donnie asked him if he wanted him to come along, Hugh didn't respond.

March 1967

8

All the boys called Martin Attunale Big Marty, but his wife just called him Martin. People called him and Tony gangsters, but they saw themselves as builders. Sometimes he had to off a guy or two for work, but he always felt that was in his past or at least so far ahead in the future that he didn't need to think about it much. He didn't have to do it but once every couple of months anyway, and he walked around some days thinking maybe he'd already done his last one. He didn't think of himself as a killer. The point was: nothing was what it looked like.

Marty took refuge in cards to while away the workdays, and they were best played alone. Quietly, with singular focus. Sure, it was occasionally enjoyable to sit around on Monday nights at the big table in the back of the butcher shop with a dozen or so guys, smoking cigars and playing for cash. But mostly he wanted to be home those nights, having pasta with Lila.

Ditto for gambling night. The other guys seemed to get pleasure-drunk the minute they hit the casino carpet, saw the lights and heard the sexy click of the chips, the atmosphere like a carnival and a church at the same time. But Marty hardly ever went on those casino trips. He preferred the table at the back of the butcher shop, which served as his de facto office during the day. It was enough to go there and play cards, hear their singular slap on the table like water lapping on a dock, dropped into the low conversation of maybe one or two other guys, or maybe no other guys at all. Maybe just him and solitaire and a couple of phone calls; a nice, quiet afternoon.

He liked his nights quiet, too. Lila had been with him since junior high, and they were sweet with each other, caring, and when the guys went out whoring after dinner Marty just went home. The guys knew it wasn't his thing. They called him the Family Man. Big Marty, Family Man, always home for dinner unless he was out on a job, with a sweet cream puff of a wife who was always by his side.

When he did go down to the casino, the place did things to the other guys that made him nervous. Marty watched the casino make Tony go silent, rigid, like he thought he might get caught there — like the cops or Tony's dad Ritchie could storm in at any moment and pick him off, take him out right there. Marty would try to talk to him but Tony would shrug him off, bad vibes coming off him in waves. Tony acted like he was about to come apart — not the way to go for a sotto-capo, the heir apparent. But then when Marty heard him talking about it after, Tony would always say he had a great time.

And Hugh at the casino was just scary. He'd go absolutely whenever he had a spare night, and he'd head straight for the craps or the blackjack table and plop down like a little kid under the Christmas tree, wide-eyed, speechless. He'd settle in instantly and he wouldn't get up until they made him. Sometimes Hughie won and sometimes he lost, but he always acted pulled to the tables as if by some unseen chain, and once it happened, you couldn't talk to him at all. He was lost until three, four in the morning, whenever somebody managed to pull him away.

Marty didn't want to lose himself like that. He'd grown up poor with a dad who died young, his mother on her own. She worked in a factory making women's stockings; she couldn't afford to wear them herself. Martin had worked every day but Sunday since he was 13, tall for his age and already filling out to be a big guy, when Tony's father hired him to make drinks and empty ashtrays at the card games. Once he became the man of the family, he couldn't afford to take his eye off the ball. If they needed him, he had to be ready. The only time he ever really let himself relax was late at night, drifting off into sleep.

That's why, he thought as he laid a Queen of Hearts down on a King of Spades, its soft blow the only sound in the still, pork-smelling back room on an early spring Tuesday, when he did have to go clip somebody, he liked to do it last thing, late at night. After dinner, preferably, and just before a scotch. It was really the only manageable way to conduct business.

Back when he and some other guys had to whack the diamond broker Moses Z., the timing wasn't up to them. They had to do it right after lunch, an awful setup. Marty had made calls all morning, trying to push it back, but Moses had told them he was headed to Atlantic City with his wife after close of business, and Ritchie said it couldn't wait.

So they did it during the day. And then Marty didn't feel like he could go home for dinner that night. He sat outside in his car, parked a couple houses up from his own, and watched Lila move around in the kitchen through the window over the sink. At about 9, she turned off the light and went up to bed. Only then could he let himself in the back door, climb the stairs, mutter goodnight and wait for sleep. Because you did that kind of work in the light of day, there was no way to reset yourself. You needed the sun to go down and you needed a long sleep, or else you just carried it with you everywhere until you went to bed.

Hitting on this idea changed Marty's life. Sadly, he was in his 40s before he figured it out. So he'd walked around with blood on his hands for 25 years, shocked no one else could see it, until he'd finally figured out the timing thing.

Plus there was this issue of violence, of guys thrashing around. With Moses it had involved the Meadowlands, a shovel and the trunk of Marty's new car. Now that he was 50, Marty felt he'd naturally risen to the level of 5 x 38, which is to say five rounds from a .38 caliber pistol, just standing with his feet spread wherever he was, the goner on the ground getting a serious headache, receiving rounds from Marty's gun like a gift from God. No more of this gigging with ice picks or reaching around from the back seat with the piano wire; that was for the younger guys. That was a struggle; that was messy. For instance, Moses' death was supposed to be bloodless, but it wasn't. When Ralphie, a junior guy but somebody Marty had thought knew what he was doing, reached around the front seat from the back with the wire around Moses' neck, he'd hit a vein or something. Blood was everywhere in seconds, all over Marty's new car. He knew in that moment that things had to change. He needed a new plan. And once he'd gotten it in place, once he'd learned to tell Tony exactly when and how he'd do that kind of work, things started to go more smoothly.

Marty's new *modus operandi* made him like his work — his daily routine, the back-and-forth with the other guys, his whole life — better. Because it wasn't like you could talk about this kind of stuff over dinner or cards or anything. You did that stuff alone, even if someone else was in the car with you, someone who'd helped you plan the whole hit; even if he'd been at your wedding and you'd spent Sunday at his kid's christening; didn't matter. When the time came to do the actual thing, you and the guy you were with didn't look at each other; you were moving together through the same space, yet you were each alone.

Then the next day you might hang out all afternoon with the same guy you did the job with, but you couldn't talk about it much. You couldn't really mention the event at all except in jokes and code. The last one they'd done, a guy they only called "the little Jew," took three guys to get into the trunk even after Marty had shot him six times. The next day, driving around with Ricky Lovano, Marty avoided conversation about it, but Ricky was still punch-drunk from he night before, couldn't get over the trouble the dead man had given them. He showed Marty the bruise on his forearm, a welt the size of a walnut, while he drove around town.

But mostly guys just didn't mention that sort of thing. So you couldn't think things through; you couldn't process. You had to find your own way of doing things or you'd lose your marbles.

So when Marty sat there on a Tuesday with Tony, they didn't talk about much. Marty knew Tony was getting keyed up about the medical school thing, but he talked around it, discussed details here and there, never getting to the gist.

Finally Tony stood up, crossed the room to icebox, said, "che peccato," as he grabbed a can of Ballatine. He held it by two fingers and swung it in the direction of the card table because it was cold and so was he. He didn't say what he was talking about, and it could've been anything. So Marty just waited while Tony sat and drank the beer like it was his job.

"There's something I can't figure out," he finally said.

Marty cut the cards.

"He's in the meeting with these statehouse guys, right?"

"Who?" Marty asked, even though he figured it was probably Hugh.

"Hugh. He's in the meeting with these statehouse guys, right? Tommy Manicotti and Al somebody, from down south. And you can tell, right when they get in the door, they don't like him. Now them — they're no great shakes, don't get me wrong. No great shakes at all. Take, for instance, the way they both dress. Garish. Unkempt like they're garbage collectors. Awful."

Marty had gotten stuck on somebody having the last name Manicotti, but said nothing.

"And Hugh starts talking to them about the medical school. And they give him the high hat."

"This surprises you?" Marty said, softly, shuffling.

"No," Tony said. "What surprised me was what Hugh did. He just sat there. He just sat there and he didn't say nothing. He just waited. It was like he was there for his Christmas presents, or something. He just waited. He just sat there and listened to them talk and then before anybody knew it they were like, okay, listen, we'll make this work for you. It'll happen."

"When was this? Were you there?" Marty cut in.

"No, I wasn't, but Hugh told me about it."

Marty shrugged, kept shuffling.

"He has a way," he finally said.

"Damn if he doesn't," Tony said. "He expected things to go his way. And they did. It's a talent, is what it is."

Marty nodded.

"That it is, my friend."

And then both men were silent for awhile, Marty lost in his thoughts. He kept picturing this weird thing that Tony always did whenever they were at lunch. Tony had this thing with service people: everything they brought him, he always tried to get a little extra. For instance, when Tony ordered a sandwich on a roll, he asked the girl making it to scoop out the extra bread in the middle, put some extra meat in there, something the other guys weren't getting. If the guys were at an Italian place, he'd call the waiter over and try to work out getting the antipasto for free. Stuff like that.

Tony was nice enough to his friends and associates. Didn't cut in on conversations, wasn't always trying to be a big man — God knew there were plenty of guys around like that. Tony's thing had to do with anybody he seemed to see as in a lesser position in life. Take, even, when he got the car filled up, he'd lean out the window and ask the guy to give him a little more at the end, after the pump had stopped — how Tony thought the attendant was ever going to do this, Marty didn't know, because they never did. It was like he was trying to prove to the world he was special through every sandwich, every tank of gas. Now here was Tony admiring Hugh for getting special treatment without ever having to ask for it.

"It's probably how he got to be mayor," Tony finally said.

Marty sat back in his chair, folded his hands over his big stomach.

"It's probably how he'll get to be governor," he replied.

"That's a fact," Tony said. He drained his beer. "With any luck, that's a fact."

May 1967

9

Donnie sat at dinner at Fontanella's downtown, bent over a steak that looked like a human heart. It was his birthday. He was 29.

Clara and his sister Doris sat with him, both looking lovely with short wavy hair and simple dresses, at an intimate table in the corner with a candle in the middle. The women were drinking wine.

"I'll just have water," Donnie had told the waiter, a tall Italian in a white shirt and thin mustache who stood neatly tucked into the heavy brocade that half-hid every table from one another. Clara and Doris looked at him quizzically, but didn't question him.

He shrugged as if he were being interrogated. "It's a weeknight. I want to keep my head clear."

Fontanella's was an institution, dark and silent but for the occasional scraping of cutlery, everything surrounded by soft curtains and plush rugs that sucked up all the secrets from its customers' conversations. There were too many forks on the table, and nobody in Donnie's party knew how to use them all. They could all afford to be there, but they generally went to lesser restaurants, or ate at home. Donnie's birthday dinner was the most expensive thing any of them had done in years.

Doris was saying something about how he should marry Clara. She said it whenever the three of them were together. Doris had been married since she was 19; that was how she thought things were supposed to go.

"You two are young. You like to work, that's fine," Doris said, buttering her roll. "But you're getting older now. It's time to think about family, that's all."

Clara smiled and nodded.

"I don't know, though. Donnie works so much. Til late every evening and then even on the weekends, sometimes. I never see him," Clara said. "Maybe we'll do it when we're ready to have children. We'll get a bigger place, you know. We'll do it when we're more ready."

Doris pointed her butter knife at Clara.

"Remind me: How old are you now?" She was the sort of person who said things like that.

Clara recoiled, but just a bit.

"I'm 30. Thanks for asking," she said, then tucked into her baked potato.

Both women snuck looks at Donnie while they talked, speaking slowly to leave gaps for him to jump into the conversation. He stared down at his steak. It was so large he had to really think about the best way to cut it up. He had a headache.

"Honestly, I don't know why all my girlfriends are so gung-ho about getting married," Clara said quietly. "Donnie makes good money, and so do I. I'd hate to give up any of that."

Clara took an audible breath, then added, "I like working, most of the time."

Donnie knew that last line was a lie. Dominic Santoro was a thug whose hatred got the best of him on most days. Clara lived for breaks and lunch these days; she'd told him that.

But getting married and moving out to the suburbs was something Donnie couldn't discuss yet. He didn't want to look into the future and see a big house with a lawn; he wanted to live in the city and walk to work, at least for now. He had to hold Clara off until he could figure out how to deal with what was going around him downtown, right now, this week.

He clutched at his water glass. His day had been so busy there had been no time to get up and go get a drink from the fountain. When Donnie got back to his desk from the one trip to the men's room that he'd managed that Monday, he found the girls from secretarial pool had remembered his birthday with a cruller and a candle on his desk chair that he very nearly sat on. Luckily, it wasn't lit.

He'd always told Clara everything. When people did interesting things at City Hall during the day, he'd file them in his mind to share with her at home at night. Sometimes she'd get fired up about what he was telling her, sometimes not, but she always showed at least a polite interest until lately.

Now things were happening at work that he didn't know how to talk about. There was nowhere to start, and he couldn't see the end. No: it was almost like a pit. Everything seemed like it was starting to lead downward. So tonight he had to watch every word; he didn't really know what to say to either Doris or Clara.

Yes, there was the church. The Immaculate Heart of Mary, built in 1922. Of course Hugh wasn't going to tear down the Immaculate Heart of Mary to make room for the medical school. Now he wanted to tear down everything across the street. To give Seton Hall 125 acres, Hugh wanted to knock down the Fairmount Houses. He had to move 500 families. And Donnie had to help.

Donnie had spent that afternoon at City Hall with Bob Walker of the Congress of Racial Equality. The man was stout and bald in a crisp white dress shirt. His face was so round and full that if he hadn't been colored, Donnie might have thought he was Italian. Bob pulled up a chair across from Donnie and sat just staring at him while Donnie explained what they were going to do. Tear down the Fairmount Houses. Move 500 families.

He'd met Walker before, several times. They were around the same age. Walker was quiet and fair, a calming presence even as he walked around downtown each week with angry Negro families holding picket signs. The last time Donnie had seen him was back in March, when Marcus White died. Walker was with the 50 people who stormed the steps of City Hall the night Santoro's cops shot the 17 year-old as he stood with friends in front of a store. The cops said the boy had put his hands in his pockets as they walked up, as if going for a gun. But Marcus didn't have a gun, just a comb. He was dead before the ambulance arrived.

Bob didn't have much to say about the Fairmount Houses situation. He acted as though he were merely collecting details for reporting to some other authority. Donnie knew he'd go right over to the site after meeting with him and start letting everybody in those buildings know what was up. Those people were going to be furious, and rightfully so.

He realized he'd been trying to cut his steak with a butter knife at the same moment Clara reached over with the proper tool, a serrated-edge scythe that seemed out-of-proportion large like everything in this restaurant — the pepper shaker was the size of a toddler and heavy enough to use as a weapon. Donnie felt himself recoil from the steak knife. Clara didn't notice; she was still trying to keep up a conversation with his sister, asking about her husband, her house, her sons.

"Boys. Hellions," Doris said, shaking her head and draining her wine at the same time. At 8 and 10, Dominic and Anthony were cute, but they seemed bent lately on loud yelling, cops and robbers and destruction of property.

"You two do get married and have kids, don't have boys. I had to fish a plastic pistol out of the toilet this morning before I went to work," Doris shook her head. "It's that kind of thing."

"What about Paulie?" Clara said, asking after Doris' husband, a lawyer who commuted to Trenton, whom they hardly ever saw.

Doris set her glass down resolutely.

"Gone by 7 a.m. everyday, of course," Doris said. "Gone by sunup and not home til after the boys are in bed. I think the gun was in there when he went to work and he never even noticed. But that's Paulie."

Donnie realized that if he looked up every few minutes and raised his eyebrows at Doris, she'd think he was paying attention. Whether Clara knew what was really going on inside his mind or not, he didn't know.

President Johnson had gone on TV back in the summer, declaring War on Poverty in his halting drawl, signing health legislation and joking with Truman that he'd better sign up for insurance now and beat the crowds. Everything had seemed about to change. It seemed to Donnie people had had enough of whole families coming up to Newark from the South for jobs and then just as quickly falling off the map.

"From the test of these days we shall emerge as a stronger nation," Johnson had drawled from his spring press conference at the ranch, as they demonstrated down in Selma.

But Johnson's big bill hadn't changed much yet. Those people would still be out there tomorrow morning in the frigid cold, glaring at Donnie while he walked to work. Men who knew he worked in the mayor's office, following him there yelling at him about how he should be doing more. Women staring up at him from filthy stoops as he walked by, holding sick kids who should have been in school.

"Donnie. I came in from Plainfield, for God's sake," his sister finally said. "I'm going to have to pay the babysitter extra."

Clara reached across the table and squeezed Donnie's hand, but her eyes were hard.

"What's eating you?" Doris said.

"Just work," Donnie said, looking back down at his plate. "It's really very difficult right now."

Both women waited. Donnie set the knife down and took a big breath.

"I think the thing is, I don't have the problems I thought was going to have," he started slowly. "I don't think people really know the difference between federal government and city government. They don't realize we don't have much access to federal money. I think they see me in a suit on my way to work, and they think I'm headed there to go spend up the money that President Johnson sent up from DC to help them get doctors and jobs."

Clara nodded.

"The medical school," she said.

"The medical school," Donnie agreed.

"That was in the paper," Doris said. "It's moving to Newark, right? Big new building. I meant to ask you about that."

Donnie nodded at his plate.

"Here's what people do understand," he said, "that my boss isn't the president, it's the mayor. And the mayor is building a big new medical school."

Doris and Clara waited for him to explain why that was a problem.

"We need it. We need that school there. There still aren't enough doctors to help the people who live here now. They're constantly coming into the office and complaining. They bring their sick kids in. This is how we fix that problem."

But he stopped there. He didn't want to tell them yet what he had to tell Bob Walker today, that so many families were going to have to move again. Because the mayor's contractor friends building more and bigger buildings and forcing colored families to move every three to four years, more or less against their will, was all just part of the plan. That this was his job now, like it or not.

"I know we need a new medical school. I can't remember a time when everybody at City Hall wasn't worried about that place," he said. "It's the state's only source of doctors and dentists, but it's been limping along since the first."

Clara and Doris just waited for him to go on, so he did.

"With that place it's like every day brings some new threat, and then the dean and the president both kicked the bucket within a week of each other last year over the Christmas holidays," he said. "The boys in Jersey City just spent the last two years running it into the ground, giving all their friends jobs. The Archdiocese — they just sort of wring their hands and look away."

Doris raised her eyebrows and left them up.

"I didn't know," she said. "Sounds like God himself gave up on it."

"So the school hasn't run in the black the whole time it's been in Jersey City?" Clara said.

"It's Jersey City," Donnie said. "They run the whole town like a sandbox full of money and they roll around in it like little kids."

Now Clara and Doris were staring at him. He felt almost like he'd overstepped in the conversation, but didn't know when or how. He'd only managed a few bites of the steak, despite being so hungry he was almost seeing spots. He tucked into it, tried to focus on it, before it went cold.

After a beat, Doris and Clara went on to other topics, and he tuned them out for awhile. When he looked up, the steak almost gone, they were staring at him.

"What?" he said.

"Doris asked if the mayor got you donuts for your birthday," Clara said gently. "Doesn't he do that sometimes?"

"Yeah," Donnie said, draining the last of his water. "I got a donut."

Wednesday,
July 12, 1967

10

Every day was a fight for the same hot, wet space. Not just good jobs and enough light in the projects that you could see where you were going at night, enough to avoid the junkies who wanted to jump you. It wasn't just about that. It was about physical space in the city, and whether you were black or white you felt it every single time you stepped out into the street.

Take a walk to the corner store for milk and first thing you'd be looking around to see who you were there with, the tension so thick you started feeling it soon as you woke up in the morning. It was in every interaction, in the split second as people first looked at you, that they might answer with a simple hello and a blank look or start yelling or not respond at all. Or they would try to kill you. You had to know where you were and who else was coming, and you had to be ready.

Whether or not they knew it, the white cops used this idea of space to their own advantage every day. They were all so big and broad-chested it sometimes looked like the very fact they existed was an attempt to take up all the available air.

The cops drove big police cars, new Plymouth Furies redesigned from the year before to be so much longer than absolutely necessary, tanks of blue and chrome that they used to chase after absolutely nothing. All their cruisers had air conditioning, so they were the only ones in the city who could get cool. You'd think they'd just want to stay in there.

They drove so fast kids had to jump back out of the way all day, and then they parked those things wherever they wanted. They were always out cruising the more law-abiding streets, staying clear out of the projects where all the crime actually went down. They'd stop you in the middle of the street sometimes, jump out waving crap-colored nightsticks, two of them at a time, instantly taking the place over with their big Italian bodies, yelling and waking everybody up.

John Simmons Smith was thin, wiry; everyone in his family was. Small and dark, easily hidden in the lack of light until he got behind the wheel of the car and turned on the Safety Cab Company sign. On the night in question it was so hot he wore nothing over light pants but a white t-shirt and drove from his house in the Central Ward downtown, the windows down as far as they would go, driving a little faster than he should to feel a little air over his body. Then he came to a police cruiser double-parked right in front of him. They did it all the time, and Smith thought little of it. No one else was coming so he just went around.

Before he completed his maneuver, they were there. They were Vito Corelli and John De Santis, a longtime pro and a six-month rook-ie, but Smith never knew who they were beyond One and Two. He wondered later where they'd come from — they were there so fast it seemed like they must have been crouched down in front of the cruiser, waiting for him.

One of the cops slammed his nightstick down on the roof of Smith's car. The first hit made him jump and stopped his heart, but the second and third ones were more rhythmic, as though the officer were pound-ing out a song on the hood.

Smith took a long, slow breath of stale air, gripped the steering wheel, stared straight ahead. The one kept beating on the car and the other came around to the driver's side, leaned down as though he would whisper to Smith or kiss him, and then screamed in his ear.

"License! Now!"

Smith reached into his back pocket for his wallet.

"Whoa! Whoa!" the officer yelled. "The fuck you reachin' for?"

The cop had to lean in to hear Smith, whose voice came out low and calm. Smith would not remember any of it, but this was the moment that he started to feel like they might want to kill him. He measured out his words like he would with unruly children. If he yelled back, the sound might rise up with the heat and burst his heart.

"I'm getting my wallet. I am getting my wallet."

They didn't hear that because they were both on him then.

Officer Vito Corelli swung open the driver's side door and grabbed Smith's t-shirt, jerking him up so his head hit the top of the car as they pulled his body out the window. Smith jerked and twisted in the other direction, his feet crawling out over the passenger seat, digging his heels in, trying to inchworm his way out the passenger side door.

Officer John De Santis kept beating on the hood with his nightstick, watched Corelli struggle with Smith on his side of the car, then decided he'd better jump in or catch hell for it later. He leaned in on the passenger side and grabbed Smith's feet and yanked on them like he was shaking out a blanket, ricocheting Smith's body against the dashboard. Now Corelli had Smith's head and he shook Smith's body the other way. They had him. It was easy.

But Smith kept kicking, so DeSantis let go. Corelli had him by the neck now, pulled him out of the car and onto the street, dropped him there. Now the cars were three deep around them, and DeSantis came around and gave Corelli cover as his partner beat Smith on the ground.

Smith's body jerked back and forth almost like a seizure, and it subsided before Corelli was ready to stop going at him. By the time the nightstick stopped coming down on Smith, he was already lifeless.

"Corelli," DeSantis said his partner's name softly, thinking he'd look up to catch a breath and stop. Corelli didn't hear him, kept beating Smith.

"Corelli!" DeSantis yelled, feeling a jolt of fear go through him. "That's enough. Stop it now."

The two men had been together since DeSantis had joined the force back after Christmas. The 40 year-old Corelli had grown up in the Central Ward, a fixture on the force since his 19th birthday, an old hand to jokey, shakey, wide-eyed DeSantis, 25. They'd done stuff like this before: stopping colored kids as they went around corners, one cop on either side, yelling at the perp into each of his ears until he just gave up the ghost and let them take him downtown. For not being respectful to them. For not answering their questions audibly enough. For nothing.

And not just kids: young, old, men, women, didn't matter. They were usually up to no good around here, Corelli had told DeSantis as they trained him up. But it had never gone this far before, not in De-Santis' first six months. He'd thought this might be coming, and now here it was, and the horror settled in DeSantis' gut while Corelli beat Smith, who didn't move at all now.

Corelli was bent over, breathing heavy from heaving the nightstick, and brought his arm down to rest, crouched like that. That's when DeSantis noticed that a small crowd had gathered on the street, and people were yelling at them.

DeSantis looked around and realized there was nowhere for any of the people to go: there was the original parked car, the cop cruiser dou-ble-parked next to it, and Smith's cab next to that. Smith's doors were both open now and two more cars had pulled up behind the cruiser. There was no way to get around all the cars in the street even if you were on foot.

DeSantis stared at the side of Corelli's head until he too finally seemed to hear all the yelling. But Corelli didn't respond, he just nod-ded at DeSantis and jerked his head back toward the cruiser. He want-ed DeSantis to open the back door and then help him get Smith inside. Corelli picked up Smith's torso with both hands and swung around to the driver's side, hauled his body in like a sack of laundry, then nod-ded at DeSantis again to go around to the other side and pull Smith in across the back seat. Then they both jumped back into the cruiser. They left Smith's car where it stood.

Corelli fired up the engine, wouldn't look at the crowd, now inches away from the front of the car. DeSantis had to jump back out, wave his arms, yell at them to get out of the way.

Corelli gunned it to the 4th Precinct, gripping the wheel, silent. DeSantis stared straight ahead as long as he could, then dared himself to look in the back at Smith. Smith lay there not moving.

"Corelli," De Santis whispered. "He's not moving. Is he dead?"

Corelli stared straight ahead.

"I don't know. I'm just drivin'."

De Santis looked back over his shoulder at Smith in the back seat until he couldn't anymore, then whipped back around.

"Shit. He's not moving."

Corelli worked his fingers around the wheel like he was strangling it.

"I told you. I'm just drivin,'" he hissed.

Then as they passed under a streetlight, DeSantis could see Smith was breathing. The relief flooding through him made him feel like he might pass out. He couldn't think what might happen to them both if Smith was dead.

They'd done a lot of crooked shit for sure. Corelli had told his new partner just as they'd started patrolling together: you have to be careful with these colored people. They're not going to be satisfied with just fair treatment. They don't have jobs, they're all on drugs, but they think they're better than us.

It looked like Corelli's neck was locked into place, the muscles taut and hard. De Santis emulated him, watched all the buildings fly by on the way to the station, not wanting to turn back around and look at Smith.

Then they were there, and DeSantis realized anew that the station was right across from Brick City — the Hayes Houses, the hulking high-rise project that the mayor's office talked about closing down but hadn't managed to yet, junkies and muggers in all the stairwells of ten different dark, scary gray buildings blotting out the horizon.

A group of men stood on the sidewalk, fixing the cruiser with their eyes, watching it pull up in front of the precinct, ready for whatever. One had a bottle and another had a stick. They watched the cruiser like they'd been waiting for it their whole lives.

One measly light bulb lit the front of the precinct, but the rest was dark. The city never fixed lights around the Hayes Houses, so every night, the very public face of the precinct was a no-man's land. De Santis never could understand it.

De Santis stared at the crowd of men, his body ready for confrontation. He sat up in the seat and reached out the window to grab the cruiser's hood, an outward show of strength from right there where he sat. Second by second he put off having to get out of the car and drag the lifeless man in the back seat up the stone steps and into the station.

If Corelli noticed his partner's sitting-fighting stance, he didn't register it. He threw the cruiser into park and jumped out and around, as if doing it all fast would keep them from trouble. De Santis sat still for one more moment, trying to fix the men on the street with his eyes, pin them to the spot where they stood. Corelli opened the driver's side back door, took a quick look at Smith, then stepped back to stare at DeSantis through the cruiser's side window.

"Well?" Corelli barked at him, "What the hell? You going to help me or what?"

De Santis threw his body against the passenger side door, sick to his stomach, hating Corelli in that moment. Then he hopped up onto the street, flipped around and opened the back door. He was trying now to psyche himself up and forget about the men staring at them from across the street for the time it was going to take to get Smith out of the car, up the steps and into the station. He didn't allow himself to think about what might happen once they got inside. You can't just bring a dying man into the station like it's nothing. You can't do that and keep your job. Even if you were white. Even if you were Italian. Even DeSantis knew that.

He pulled on Smith's legs and Corelli came around from the other side and got ready to pick up his torso, to take Smith out just the way he went in. Smith was definitely either passed out or dead. De Santis' gut flipped over and he thought he'd throw up standing there holding the man's legs.

He couldn't resist looking up again at the men across the street. They seemed to have expected Smith to get out of the car by himself. When it was clear the officers were trying to handle a man who might be dead, they started marching toward the car like they owned it. They circled and started to yell. De Santis was never able to make out many words. The blood rushing in his ears was loud, and he wanted to cover his ears with his hands, but he couldn't because they were still holding Smith by the feet. The man's body was heavy as a piano, funny for such a slight guy, and both cops were breathing hard and stumbling well before they got him up to the steps. Thank God then some of the men came out from inside the station and met them there. They all got a piece of Smith and carried him quickly up and in.

DeSantis kept his eyes on the ground, and they found the feet of Dominic Santoro, his chief. For a second he wondered, his mind wild, if he'd be fired on the spot. If Santoro would just take out his weapon and shoot him through the head, throw his body out the back door with Smith's, cover the whole thing up. Because you can't just beat a guy to death just because he's in your way and he's a Negro. Right?

Santoro waited, arms akimbo, for them to set the lifeless man down on a bench and straighten up before whisper-shouting into Corelli's ear: "The fuck you bring him here for?"

That's right, DeSantis thought, relieved. This is not my thing. This is Corelli's thing. It's Corelli went apeshit on the guy. Not me.

But Corelli seemed struck dumb. DeSantis straightened up, staring at his partner, feeling the allegiance he'd built over six months peel off him like a strip of dead wallpaper under a chisel, just like that.

Meanwhile, the chief's eyes were bugging out: "Is he even...fuck-ing...alive?"

As if in answer, over on the bench, Smith twitched and tried to sit up. All dozen cops in the room stared like he was a ghost. Smith lay back down and passed out again.

"The hospital," Santoro hissed. "Now. Out *that* door," and he pointed down the hallway to the back door, where there was a little light, at least.

Then the brick crashed in through the window of the dispatcher's office. Then everything went to hell.

II

James Cash came out the Hayes Homes front doors, heavy metal and glass contraptions so dirty they felt coated in the humid muck of the night. They were gummy to the touch. And there on the steps, spilling out into the street, were most of the people he'd met in his life. And about a hundred more.

Some of them looked around to see him, but most faced away, their heads turned up to watch what was happening in the police station directly across the street. It was incongruous at first — with that many people gathered together, you'd expect yelling. But it was so quiet, the only sound murmuring and clinking glass. At first it was hard to tell where the clinking sound was coming from, there were so many people around. James smelled gasoline and burning rubber, fumes like a car fire coming from somewhere. He couldn't see much. Darkness nearly overwhelmed the few streetlights that were still operational.

He locked eyes for a second with his cousin Eugenia, two years older, saw the unbuttoned top of her light cotton dress fall away from her collarbone, her sweat there catching what little light came from the poles above the station. He wanted to warn her away, but she'd gotten there first. Shouldn't she warn *him*, about …whatever was happening here?

He caught sight of his brother Fred, holding a broken bottle and pacing. Fred's friends stood around him, talking, their arms rising and falling as though they were marching somewhere. James registered them, but he didn't go over to them, didn't ask them why they were there.

Something was bad wrong. The crowd said that with all its bodies, in numbers that seemed to double in the few minutes James spent trying to figure out how many were there. They moved all around him, all arms and sweaty legs and feet on the gravelly street, swiveling their heads to stare up at the station. They milled around and started getting loud, pointing up at the broken window, its jagged panes like pointy black teeth in a shouting mouth.

Then James got sucked up into a crowd wave that picked him up where he stood on the curb and carried him across the street to the police station steps, dropping him off there like something passed out and washed ashore. Then he found his feet and blinked back sweat to try to see 30 feet up into the precinct windows. The quiet went to deafening in a second. It was like staring up from the bottom of a pit.

He thought for a minute of people he'd heard about — just in the last year — who'd been taken into that station and never came back out. People from the Central Ward.

Last spring, Lester Long got stopped by the cops for a traffic violation and ended up dead two hours later. Lester grew up around the corner from James. He was only 22 when he died. Last Christmas Eve, the cops were searching 17-year-old James Mathis when somebody's gun went off and he got shot.

Just this past spring, Bernard Rich got taken to jail for some reason nobody knew and was never seen alive again. Bernard had just turned 26; James had been with him on his birthday.

James blinked back the start of tears, tried to get his bearings.

Now the front doors opened and a dozen cops came out, holding their arms out from their sides, scuttling down the precinct stairs. They spread their hands to show they didn't have nightsticks. Most of them moved their arms around them in an attempt to sweep people back from the precinct stairs. There's nothing to see here, some of them said. It's time to go home.

We are home, some people said. You get out.

James stood on his toes, staring at the station, when something, a brick or a bottle, sailed from behind him over his head and went right through one of the windows. It made just a clink in the wet night.

Then behind him was somebody he didn't know holding another bottle, this one clear and filled with brown liquid that looked like whiskey, but as James looked closer he saw was actually turpentine and dish soap and whatever else goes into a Molotov cocktail — Fred had told him all about them, back when he was demonstrating on a more regular basis, but he'd never actually seen one. Did they have that ready, waiting in somebody's kitchen to bring out tonight? Had people been planning this for weeks? What was happening? Then that bottle flew over his head too, exploding into a flash of fire on the building's cornerstone.

That's when James noticed cops moving, fast. If they were outside, they ran inside. A few from the inside ran outside, looking back over their shoulders for flames in the windows. They were bent over, running like rats with their tails on fire.

For a second, James couldn't figure out where he was. One second he was standing in front of the building that had been his own home for years. It was across from the back of the police station, but he'd almost forgotten that — the cops rarely used the entrance that faced the Hayes Homes. So for the last year or so, the only time James really saw cops was at work, at City Hall. He felt like slapping himself, right there on the street, realizing that these were the same guys he'd casually cross to the other side of the hall to avoid at work. Their building was on fire, and his people were making it all happen.

James watched people walk or run back to the Hayes Homes, his eyes adjusting to the lack of light until he could see just as well as daytime. He saw movement up on top of the building, twelve stories up. People were throwing rocks and bottles at police they saw on the ground.

He jumped when a rock split against the ground with a chalky thud, and watched as the last of the cops scuttled back inside. Seconds later, James looked around, didn't see a single officer.

People he knew from the neighborhood were rushing to the scene, running up to him to find an eerie quiet.

"They've got him in there!" somebody shouted, answering James's thoughts. He whipped his head toward the voice.

Who, James formed the word with his mouth and looked around, but didn't speak out loud. He heard the smash of another bottle, looked around to see where it had come from. The lights started going out inside the station, like the cops in there were trying to hide.

"WHO?" James shouted now, at anybody who would answer. It turned out Eugenia was right behind him. She told him about John Smith, the cab driver. That they'd dragged him into the station an hour ago, and people were saying he might be dead.

Something made James look back over his shoulder at his and Lena's building, but it was so tall he'd never thought to count windows from the street and see which one might be hers, and so much was going on now he'd never find her window. He probably wouldn't see her even if she was leaning out that window now, craning her neck to watch him from above.

"Where is Bob?" a woman cried from behind him. "I thought I saw Bob, but now I don't know where he is."

The woman asked her question a few more times over the next five minutes, as James stared back down at the ground to rest his neck. Her question was met with murmurs from people in the the crowd who hadn't seen Bob. Then someone said they'd seen Bob go into the station.

Then it was like in a dream, where you suddenly know something you didn't before. James realized the woman had been talking about Bob Walker. And he finally knew why everyone was there, and what they were going to do now.

Should he warn Lena, wake up her parents? He hoped the whole family was asleep, didn't know about what was going on down here.

Fifteen floors was high up. Whatever was happening down here couldn't reach her up there. And his neck started to hurt from staring up at the Hayes Homes, then whipping back around to peer through the precinct windows.

At that point, as James stood staring down at his shoes with his hand massaging the back of his neck, he heard a crash. Someone had thrown another Molotov cocktail at the precinct window. It crashed through and lit up the dark room inside with flames. There was a lot of yelling coming from inside the station, and a minute later five big cops burst through a side door, waving nightsticks this time.

James felt too close to the station. He ran back across the street and stood behind a tree next to the front doors of Lena's building, just in time to see Bob Walker come through the front door of the precinct in a white t-shirt, carrying a bullhorn, flanked by two cops. Then suddenly Fred was standing next to him, not saying anything, just looking. Neither of the brothers spoke. James felt guilty knowing why Walker was there and wondered if Fred knew. He snuck a look at his brother's face, and could tell he did know. Of course he would know.

Fred had kept right on meeting with Walker and the Congress of Racial Equality People the whole time James had been working for the mayor. But even as Fred must have known his older brother potentially had access to a lot of information about the latest doings in that office, he never asked James. And James never offered it, because he didn't have any information anyway.

So far, Donnie and the mayor had kept James well out of sight of any of the problems he'd actually been hired to help them with. Walker had just been in the office recently for a meeting with Donnie, but James hadn't found out about it until the meeting was over.

His shame was white-hot. It melted into the sounds of flying bottles and screams in the street, the sounds of people finally let loose.

Bob had made his way to a parked car in front of the station. He climbed up on the hood and took a second to steady himself. He started speaking to the crowd with the bullhorn.

"All right," he said, his words booming and bouncing off the street.

"Now I want you all to listen to me. We need to move away from here. We need to go down to City Hall. All of us, together. We need a vigil if it takes all night. We have got to start a demonstration to show the Police Department that we mean business."

He paused and a roar went up from the crowd while Walker dodged a rock. One of Fred's friends, a man about his brother's age standing nearby with a shirt buttoned up wrong and half-tucked in, said, "Start one? What does he think *this* is?"

When he stood again and spoke through the bullhorn, he held a hand over his face, palm out, shielding himself.

"Why do we need a vigil? Is he dead? Where's the cab driver?" somebody shouted up at Walker. "Where's John Smith? Is he dead?"

"He is not dead. They took him to the hospital," Walker responded, softer now but still through the bullhorn. "He is injured but he will recover."

Then he looked down at another young black man in a dirty blue t-shirt, someone James didn't know, trying to climb up onto the car with him, yelling at him at the same time.

"How do you know, man? Did you see them go? Did they take him in the back of a cop car? How do you know they went to the hospital? How do you know?"

People standing around the man pulled him back to the ground while Walker visibly gathered himself just in time to dodge another rock. Then he spread his legs to stand more solid on top of the car, stood up straight, and started shouting through the bullhorn.

"YOU'VE GOT TO LISTEN TO ME NOW. IT'S TIME TO GO. TO CITY HALL. NOW."

Then he jumped down and ran toward James, who was still standing with Fred, the two of them half-hiding behind a tree at the Hayes Homes. Walker went to the tree opposite them, steadied himself against it. Fred went over to talk to Walker but James just stared at him, wanting to help but not knowing what to say. Then another bolt of shame as James realized Walker didn't even recognize him.

Then Walker stood up straight and joined the crowd walking toward City Hall. James followed a few steps behind. He didn't know what they were all going to do when they got there.

12

The windows were open, but it wasn't doing any good. Even on the second floor with the fan in the window, Gloria lay on her side in her sweat, waiting for sleep.

She'd dozed, then awakened as Hugh came in late and slipped in next to her, home from whatever he did with the guys in back of Saul's Butcher Shop every Wednesday night. She suspected it involved cards and stiff drinks and definitely, by the sour-earth scent that sank into every piece of clothing he owned, cigars.

He lay next to her, also on his left side facing out the window, and what little humid air wafted over him carried that aroma, dark and warm but not entirely unpleasant. The worst thing was the moisture, hanging in the air all night long and turned into dew in the morning, everything coated and wet, inside and out.

Gloria tossed and turned that night, dimly aware of the fan that blew every second, of her husband starting to snore. When the phone rang downstairs in the middle of the night, she shot upright in the bed right along with him, one hand to her heart and the other to the top of her head, where the curlers pulled and hurt her shortest hair.

This happened sometimes, these calls. Not usually at one in the morning, but sometimes. Hugh swung his legs to the side of the bed and stood to put on robe and slippers, decorum important to him even in his bedroom in the middle of the night.

Hugh was downstairs long enough that Gloria fell back into fitful sleep. When she awoke again the clock said three a.m. He was still gone.

She hated to go downstairs in curlers. It made her look every bit like his mother, who didn't give a hoot what she looked like yet still had a firm hand in maneuvering everybody else in the house. Usually if you got up at three in the morning, Livia Addonizio would get up too and go downstairs and heat up ziti for you, because if you were up that late, of course you needed to eat. You obviously needed to pour a glass of wine and have a sit-down with couple of pork chops, and Livia would just put on her housecoat and slippers and trudge back and forth from the kitchen until it was all laid out in front of you, as though she'd had it all ready to go and was just waiting for you to get up in the middle of the night and eat it.

But Gloria didn't do things that way. With Gloria, dinner was at seven whether Hugh was there to eat it or not, and he usually wasn't. She'd have a sandwich or feed the children leftover spaghetti, and if he was hungry when he came home late, he could just fend for himself.

When she got downstairs, she found Hugh alone at the dining room table, feet tucked primly under the chair and hands folded in front of him, attentive, as though he was at dinner, listening to someone talk. She stopped behind him and squinted to make sure, but he was alone; no one else was there at the table with him. He didn't turn around or look at her as she walked up, so eventually she pulled out the chair next to him as if she were a guest at the same dinner party, sat down and didn't say a word for a minute.

It was just so strange. Maybe someone had died? She mentally scanned the surviving elderly family members. But if it was one of theirs, he wouldn't have just let her sleep through something like that. He would have told her. Did something happen to one of his friends, or one of their children, or Donnie, who worked in his office? There were too many possibilities.

Hugh finally, slowly, turned in his chair to face her.

"What are you doing up, Gloria?" he said softly.

"What do you mean?" She spoke as quickly as her still-sleeping mind would allow her. "I'm up because you're up. What's going on?"

Now she saw he had a book of matches in his hands. He'd been down here for two hours, sitting by himself, playing with a book of matches. He set it down on the table now and spread his hands while he talked, and she could suddenly see how at sea he was.

"The Negroes. They're at City Hall right now," He stopped then as if looking for the right word. "They're … demonstrating."

Gloria squinted again, trying to envision it.

"They're there now? Why?" she said, confused. If there was some disturbance downtown, why was he sitting there at the table alone? It was inconceivably strange.

He picked the matchbook up again, fiddled with the cover, slipping it in and out of the little cardboard lip. He shrugged a little as he told her, "I'm not sure."

*   *   *

But of course he was sure. Donnie had been clear, when he'd called two hours ago, exactly what the Negroes were doing and why.

They'd seen Dominic's boys beat up a colored cab driver and drag him unconscious into the police station. Bob Walker had come by and tried to reason with them. He'd tried to get them to calm down, and they wouldn't calm down.

Donnie called Hugh at 1:00 a.m. because the reporters from the *Times*, the *Post* and the *Evening News* had all called him at his apartment, wanting statements. Donnie said he'd gotten dressed and walked out into the street to see … bedlam. Negros running in loose, wild groups, looting stores, throwing broken bottles. Starting fires. He'd run back up to his apartment and called Hugh, who listened calmly, said he'd call back in a minute, hung up the phone, paced around the dining room.

At 1:20 a.m., Hugh called Donnie back.

"Write this down," he said. "We will issue the following statement: 'This is a difficult situation, but apparently it has no significance as far as relating to any other problem. This is an isolated incident.'"

There was silence on the other end of the phone for a minute.

"That's it?" Donnie finally said.

"That's it. We can talk about this more in the morning."

Hugh called Donnie again at a quarter 1:45.

"How do we contain this?" he asked when Donnie picked up the phone.

Donnie breathed heavily through his nose, and Hugh recognized it as the only expression of frustration his assistant would permit himself.

"Contain it?" Donnie finally said. "I don't know how we contain this. I don't know that it can be contained. This is out of control."

"Don't Dominic's boys know how to contain it?" Hugh shot back.

"Well," Donnie said, so slowly that Hugh, standing at the window with the phone in his hand, felt himself on the tip of his toes. "I think it's Dominic's boys started this whole thing. I think that's the problem."

Then Hugh hung up and called Donnie back twenty minutes later. When Donnie answered, he said: "Don't call the house again. I don't want you to wake Gloria and the children."

"Alright," Donnie said quietly.

"What are you doing now?" Hugh asked.

"I'm watching everything from my apartment window," Donnie said. "Every time I talk to you and set the phone down, reporters call."

Hugh shook his head, alone in the room.

"This must be contained," he retorted. He still held the phone with the long cord in the dining room by the window, looking out at his calm, leafy backyard in the night.

"I know that," Donnie said, "but I'm looking out my apartment window right now at a car that's been burning for half an hour, and I hear gunshots. Two guys just beat another guy up right in front of my building. I don't know how to contain this.... I think there might be snipers with guns," he went on. "Up on top of some of the buildings."

Hugh thought that sounded like Greek or Mesopotamian; it didn't make sense. Snipers? Now Donnie was saying that a couple of Dominic's boys had been taken to the hospital.

Hugh grimaced, paced, called back every twenty minutes. He wanted to eat, he didn't want to eat. Gloria had gone back to bed; she would tell him that he needed to get back to bed too, to get some rest so he could face all this in the morning. Donnie was trying to pull him back downtown, now, in the middle of the night, and he would not go. They could contain it. He could stay home for now. It would be fine.

At 4 a.m., Donnie called Hugh again, disobeying his previous order not to. He said he'd gotten word that Dominic's boys had shot two men dead, but he didn't have any official word of who the men were. He said he did get official word of Cora Miles, 28, who had come to her apartment window to look out and see what was going on at 1:30 a.m., holding her two-year old daughter in her arms. She'd been hit when a stray bullet came through her window and killed on the spot.

13

Hugh awoke the next morning to Gloria gently shaking his hip. It was 7 a.m. He'd come back to bed silently, lay in the dark staring at the box fan in the window until it was past 5:00, and then fell into a slumber that felt like being packed in a big, soft box and shipped underground, a man-size package bound up in the dark.

He looked up at Gloria, seated on the edge of his side of the bed.

"Did you sleep?" she asked.

He shrugged. He guessed so.

"Are you going downtown now?"

He squinted, nodded at her, and then realized yes, the thing to do was get there now, as soon as possible. He sat up, swung his feet to the floor, stood and moved past her, started to dress.

"Do you want coffee?" she asked, still at the edge of the bed.

He nodded again, pulling on his pants. She went to get the coffee.

He went to their bedroom window and looked out. Five newspapermen were standing on the lawn.

Coffee in hand, he waved them off as he walked to the car. He recognized them, but pretended he didn't.

"We'll call you at the office, then," one of them called to him as he passed them. He nodded and kept walking.

He'd started driving himself to the office once the family had moved out to New Shrewsbury. It was more than 30 miles from Newark and he wouldn't ask Donnie or anybody else to come and collect him every day. So he got himself a new Plymouth Fury, same deal as the cops got, and hit the Garden State Parkway every morning. Usually he listened the radio, but not today. He'd reached for the knob, then thought better of the whole enterprise. Donnie would tell him about everything when he got there.

It was just after 8 on a July Thursday morning, and already hot. Everything looked relatively normal as he swung the Fury off the Parkway and right onto Springfield Avenue for the four miles of road that would take him to City Hall. The first two miles of Springfield Avenue looked just fine. But then again, he wasn't quite sure what he was looking for.

We need a plan, he thought. No matter what, we're going to need a plan.

Then around 10th Street things started to change. Black men crossed the street quickly, some shirtless, going in different directions. Paper, cardboard, garbage was strewn in the street. The sun shone so bright it was hard to see.

This must be it, this street must be where everything had happened, because the street itself started reminding him of the war, of Dresden blown open by bombs. He thought he'd better take a side street, but instead sat for a second, transfixed by the damage, by the feeling he was driving ever closer to the center of the vacuum created by last night's explosion.

At the corner of Springfield and Bergen, large groups of people — more shirtless men, but now also women in colorful, flowery cotton dresses, grandmothers, men who should have been at work — walked the streets, staring into blown-out shop windows. They dressed in bright green, orange, navy blue untucked shirts, some from the night before, hanging limp in the heat. Children ran around and women cried on the corners with their arms crossed.

Hugh drove, eyes straight ahead, and wondered why he wasn't reacting. For a second he felt like a kid, forcing opening the closet door at night and looking right at the monster he'd known would be there. But now that he saw the monster's face, the fear turned him to stone. He could do nothing, really, but to stand there and stare at it.

Entwhistle's Dress Shop looked bombed out. There was no glass left in the window, no door left to walk through, nothing but garbage and glass and broken wooden boards on the sidewalk, no dresses in sight. Its iron gates, locked up every night by Sol Entwhistle, who'd inherited the place from his father and run it for 30 years, had been pulled apart and left to dangle on the ground like an accordion, its 12-ft. iron spikes poking out way past the sidewalk and into the street. A group of blacks stood on the sidewalk staring inside. A teenaged boy walked purposefully by, carrying a baseball bat like a baby in both arms.

Next door to Entwhistle's was the shoe store where Hugh had picked up his Florsheims in the spring. Its green-grey awning had a huge hole where someone had yanked it half off the building and left it to hang down cockeyed and broken, its metal supports exposed.

Suddenly a gunshot sounded from not too far away and nearly stopped his heart. It was then he realized the riot was still happening, and he was driving right through the middle of it. Hugh faced forward, stopped surveying the damage, gripped the steering wheel and willed himself to look straight ahead, only. He kept the car in the middle of the street, away from the sidewalk, half afraid somebody would jump in if he got too close. He waited, tense, for the light to change so he could drive forward, past the fire department and the post office, head quickly and quietly and, God help him, unnoticed up to City Hall. But the light never changed, because it was a dark mess of broken glass.

The street around City Hall was filled with smoke, ripped-up paper, bottles, discarded shoes and clothing. The smell of burning rubber wrapped around Hugh's head as he walked up to the building. A couple of black men sat on the curb and glared as he walked by, but didn't move.

All the girls in the typing pool stopped their work and watched him walk by, his heels click-clicking on the wooden floors, past their desks and through the heavy double doors into his office. He passed through the doors and closed them both behind them quietly. He turned to see that Donnie was already there, his back to the door, slumped in one of the guest chairs facing the mayor's desk. His right arm was held up by the arm of the chair and his head lay in his hand.

He said nothing, and Hugh said nothing. Hugh came around to face him, lay his briefcase on the desk, spread his hands out on it.

"All right," he said, because it didn't look like Donnie was going to speak first. Donnie seemed about to cry. "Let's have a rundown on what's gone on so far."

"Two men and one woman dead," Donnie said softly. "That we know of. So far."

Hugh gasped for air and sat down as slowly as possible.

"Dominic's boys killed two men last night. Looters. They were trying to make off with…" Donnie looked away and waved his hand tiredly. "TV sets…shoes…stuff they took out of the shops along Springfield Avenue."

Hugh was sitting now, his mouth slightly ajar, avoiding looking right at his assistant. Donnie had been with him since his inauguration, a soft-spoken, self-styled operative with a low voice that calmed the angriest Newarkers, the antsiest reporters. Hugh had never seen him shaken like this.

"The staff are …," Donnie searched for the right words. "Worried. They're worried that they're not safe here. I think we should send them home."

"Fine. And what about the press?" Hugh ventured.

"Well, they've…" and again Donnie trailed off, waved his hand before settling his forehead back into it. "They've been calling every half hour."

Hugh nodded, exhausted already.

"I gave them a statement last night," he said, shrugging.

"Yes," Donnie looked up, straight at him now. "I don't think that's going to be enough. We've got a press conference later with the governor. He wants to call in the National Guard."

"All right," Hugh breathed. If Richard Warren was coming, that meant everything was already out of control. The man Hugh was meant to replace was going to breeze in and assure everyone that the state was in control because City Hall and the police didn't know what they were doing. And Warren was going to bring National Guard boys in. They would be overrun.

"When?" he breathed.

"Soon. Today, I think," Donnie said.

Hugh's desk phone rang. Donnie leaned forward and answered without making eye contact with Hugh. He said hello and then just nodded, as if the person on the phone was in the room with them. Then he just handed the receiver to Hugh and left the room.

The young, metallic sound of the reporter's voice grated in Hugh's ear. It wasn't somebody he'd had ever spoken with before. The man — a boy really, why were did all these people asking questions suddenly seem so young? — was calling from the *Times*.

Hugh told him he'd give him a statement at the press conference. The reporter asked him what time that would be, and Hugh didn't know, because Donnie had left the room. He asked him to hold a moment so he could put the call back out to the secretarial pool, but the reporter was onto him.

"Mr. Mayor, can you comment on the effect of your choosing an uneducated white man to fill a vacant school board post has had on the current violence?"

That had happened months ago. CORE members were upset at the time, but Hugh thought of the incident as having blown over.

"I don't think that had any impact at all," Hugh said.

"But isn't it true that a qualified black man was nominated to serve on that majority-white body and that you put forward a friend of yours, who is white, instead?"

To Hugh it felt like the young man — he had a thick New England accent, really he couldn't have been more than a teen — was hurling questions at him rapid-fire as though they were out in the street and Hugh was trying to run away, instead of sitting calmly at his desk, looking out through the slats in the window at the garbage on the ground.

"I honestly don't see what that has to do with any of this," Hugh said quietly, realizing that second that to him, it was true.

He'd known Negroes his whole life. When he'd run for mayor, he'd run as everybody's friend — Irish, Jewish, Negro, it didn't matter. CORE had made it clear that they wanted jobs in his administration. So he'd hired James Cash. And there had been other appointments. He'd built buildings for them to live in. But there were so many of them, more all the time moving north for jobs he hadn't had time to create yet. And they wanted everything now, now, now.

"Well then, do you think Dominic Santoro's record of brutality has had anything to do with this uprising? Do you think it has anything to do with the fact that blacks in Newark are relegated to substandard housing, living in unsafe conditions and constantly forced by your administration to move, several times a year?"

My God, Hugh thought, he's reading from something. He's got a list.

Hugh took a breath.

"It's my understanding," Hugh retorted, "that a single man was arrested for doing something against the law, and a group of thugs gathered in front of the police station and started throwing rocks."

He forced himself to take a breath, to speak slowly, to sound more in control.

"You've got to understand," he continued. "These are not law-abiding citizens we're talking about."

"Is that why you're considering calling in the National Guard? Because one of the police captains has been shot?" the reporter shot back.

"That's not my call," Hugh said quietly, searching the closed door for Donnie. "That is the governor's jurisdiction."

"That's your comment at this point, then?"

"That's my comment."

* * *

New Jersey Governor Richard Warren was a head taller than Hugh, and younger. The papers had called him the perfect picture of Catholic New England. He arrived later that morning, and there was no confab when he'd first walked into City Hall, no sit-down in which he and Hugh compared notes and made plans. Warren sat outside the mayor's office on a bench and issued orders from there, and at 2:00 p.m. the two stood outside on the steps giving a press conference, hastily arranged and ill-equipped, as all the secretaries had been given leave to go home.

Warren stood at the podium with Hugh off to his side, the mayor marginalized right there in front of his own City Hall. He struggled to look at Warren while he spoke; Warren stood right in the front of the microphone and faced the crowd directly. He was so much taller that Hugh had to look almost completely over his left shoulder, right up into the sun, to seem attentive while Warren spoke.

The governor had the same information that Donnie had given Hugh. Apparently at Presbyterian Hospital, a few blocks away, shots had rung out all night and were continuing throughout the day. Snipers had been seen on the tops of buildings, firing randomly into crowds.

"The people in Newark have to choose sides. They are either citizens of America or criminals who would shoot down a fire captain in the back and then depend on people to speak in platitudes about police brutality," Warren sneered into the microphone to a crowd of hot reporters. "Make no mistake. This is a criminal insurrection by people who say they hate the white man, but who really hate America."

Suddenly Warren seemed to finish speaking and moved aside, making room for Hugh. They hadn't discussed any of it beforehand, and Warren made no move to lower the mic for Hugh, who had to reach up and pull the hot metal down towards his mouth and repeat what the governor had already said.

In the middle of everything, with the National Guard boys loaded onto trucks and barreling toward them from Trenton, the boy reporter called again to ask, snidely, Hugh thought, if he still thought the violence was an isolated incident. Before Hugh answered the question, he said, he wanted to let him know that he'd seen the house Hugh had grown up in — the mayor had held a press conference right in front of the place during the first election in '62, stood right there in the garden with a mic and called the whole place his — was on fire.

Hugh held the phone to his ear and felt all the air get sucked right out of the room. My God, he thought. The whole city is gone.

All he wanted was to go home, but he stayed holed up at City Hall for what seemed like forever, mostly making and getting calls. They had long, tense meetings with Santoro, Walker, Warren, deputies, policemen and reporters. The Guard moved in, 200 men in tanks and jeeps and full artillery, carrying machine guns, clearing the streets.

The secretaries filtered back into the office after the second day, escorted by Guards. Donnie moved in on the couch in his office and he and Hugh took turns peering through the slats in the blinds, waiting for things to ease up. Every few hours the phone rang and they tallied up the death count anew. Hugh called home periodically to reassure Gloria that things were fine. She asked if she should keep the children inside, he told her no, the violence seemed to be abating and at any rate was concentrated downtown. But he didn't believe what he was telling her.

On the fourth day of the riots, Hugh went back home to New Shrewsbury, commuting slowly back in each day, escorted by tanks. The looting and killing went on for two more days. In the end, 26 people were dead.

15

It was still cold out back when Big Marty started wearing the wire.

The day started out like a normal one. Tony had called him earlier that week, telling him about a sit-down scheduled in a few days to talk about hiring construction supervisors for the new medical school building. Marty knew Hugh and Tony wanted him to serve as a sort of overseer for the process with the blueprints; they'd talked about it in Puerto Rico.

The meeting took place in the conference room of an unfamiliar office building downtown. Marty smelled a rat immediately; he didn't recognize anyone in the room. It was two young guys in bad suits, Irish and Italian, seated at a tiny square table.

The Irish guy, who stood up to show he was nearly as tall as Marty, called him "Mr. Attunale," saying it to rhyme with "alley," getting the accent completely wrong. He pulled out a chair and indicated with ham hands that Marty should sit down right now, before anybody was even introduced.

Marty sat, and the Italian looked right into his eyes and put a small cassette tape down on the table.

"Do you know what that is, Mr. Attunale?"

Was this a joke?

"It's a tape. For a tape recorder. Why?"

The Italian — so small he hadn't even gotten up when Marty came into the room, as if he didn't want his friend to know that Marty could've crushed him easily — took the tape back, put it in his pocket. He looked like he maybe didn't get enough food when he was a kid.

"That's a tape of one of your friends, Angelo DeCarlo. Talking about paying off the mayor to fix a bunch of deals on this new building project of his. Know anything about that?"

Marty's heart hurt.

"I work as a construction supervisor for a reputable company," he said smoothly. "I don't know nothing about tapes."

"Do you know Angelo DeCarlo?" the big Irishman said.

"I'll tell you who I don't know," Marty began, "is you people."

"Oh. Well. We're federal agents," the little one said, and Marty felt he'd known it all along.

They started talking about Marty wearing a wire pretty straightaway.

That first morning he had to put it on himself, locked in the bathroom trying to work with the smallest possible sliver of duct tape, right there at the top of his chest where the hair wasn't quite so thick. He clipped it to his t-shirt right at the neck, where it held onto the seam like a grasshopper. Then he just covered the wire with a sweater, and then wore a leather jacket on top of the whole thing, and Marty was a big man, so no one knew.

That first day with the wire had been like going in for surgery, like lying down and baring yourself to knives that would creep in during your sleep and slice your arteries up, no chance to defend yourself. He was so big already, so used to cutting a wide swath through the air, and the contraption under his sweater made him feel thicker, and yet more breakable. He instinctively held his arms away from it, and they hung down useless at his sides.

He was always one to get up in the morning and shower and shave, try to look nice, and that always took some time. After awhile, clipping the wire to the t-shirt was almost like just one more hygienic duty, like shaving, except that it made his stomach lurch every time. His stomach so big he couldn't see his feet, filled with pasta and scotch and wine.

The day he traipsed downtown to get the wire, after walking out of the New Jersey State Detectives Office on Centre Street feeling like a bomb was strapped to his chest, Marty went to Jackie's Restaurant with Ralphie and Tony, and ate and drank like it was his last night on earth. He imagined trying to reinstall the godforsaken thing in the morning, holding the little clip between his big, soft fingers and hoping it didn't spring away and fly across the room or something. In the back of his mind, back behind the big talk and the booze, was the vague hope he just wouldn't wake up.

But he did, and he wore the thing for months, every day clipping it to his t-shirt, covering it over with a bulky sweater. People would talk to him and his right hand would want to float up with a mind of its own to feel the place where it hid underneath his clothes, afraid of the bump that he kept so close to his neck he was afraid to reach over to pick anything up off the desk or the floor. It felt like a weight pulling his head down, and he stood stick-straight to compensate. But he was getting older, so even that hurt. His big belly had been with him for a decade. Lately, it was always aching.

And it was summer now. Hot. It took him an extra 10 minutes every morning to hide the wire.

His knees were starting to not work anymore. As he came down the stairs in the morning, they'd give way seconds too soon, leaving him perched on the top step, wavering, suddenly unsure where his body was in space. His knees would just jut out to the side like they were running his body's whole show, reminding him there were bones under there, under all the fat and hair, bones that were rebelling right there on the stairs and threatening to throw him down.

So he slowed up, but that didn't help. This morning, there on the top step, the right knee buckled under him, and he bent his neck to stare down at his belly even though he knew he wouldn't be able to see his knees from there. Just tilting his head made him think for a split second that the wire might rise up and slap him in the face. So he lifted his head, stared straight into the middle distance, and made himself slow down, one step at a time staring straight ahead, painfully lowering his whole water buffalo-like body down the flight of stairs, trying to avoid bouncing off the wall or the banister, his heart rate rising so much with the effort that he started to hear waves in his ears, and here he was just trying to get down the goddamned stairs.

Lila was reading the paper at the table, already dressed, looking like a million bucks in a blue pantsuit, wavy brown hair brushed and curled, red lipstick. By the time he got to the bottom step she was staring, frowning at him. He thought it was because she'd watched him the whole time, was concerned about him.

But instead she said, "Are you going downtown today? There's rioting down there, Martin! It's not safe. Tell me you can stay home today?"

Riots? No. He couldn't stay home today. He thought he'd told her this out loud, but it was all in his mind. They just stared at each other for a second, and then he just shook his head at her. She started to open her mouth but he held up his hand. She looked back to the paper.

The FBI guys had actually never told him not to tell his wife about the wire. Most of his friends didn't talk to their wives at all, and most of them had girlfriends they didn't tell anything to either, those girls never knew a thing about any of them.

No way could he tell her. No way. And since he couldn't tell her about the wire, he had stopped telling her much about anything at all.

Today he just stood at the base of the stairs for what felt like a half hour, then waved to her as if he was way across the room. He marched past her like he was the plumber come to work on the toilet, like he didn't know her, and headed for his coffee and the red.

Oh-ho, the red. Lila had started whining back when it was still cold out that she wanted a new kitchen. The one they had worked fine for him but oh no, she said, it was drab. Painted blue from back when they bought the house, grey carpet, grey painted cupboards, no personality!, she said.

"Can we get some cheer in here, Martin?" she sang one weekend, pointing a red fingernail at the scratched countertop. "Let's make this red!"

Firehouse red, the red of her fingernails. She produced one of the magazines she took every month, *House Beautiful*. The kitchen she pointed to in the magazine spread, it looked like someone had taken fifty bottles of her red nail polish and squirted them at this kitchen through a firehose.

No, Marty thought now, blood. It reminded him of blood. Except blood wasn't like paint, it didn't stick to the paintbrush, it coated your whole arm the second you touched it. Once you saw that much blood out in the open, it was all over. Lila looked at that red and saw good things, things like her own pretty fingers, and he looked at it and thought about killing people. And by Christmas, they'd had a blood-red kitchen that he had to face every time he wanted coffee.

He walked into it today, already eighty degrees at 8:00 in the morning, and he couldn't breathe for second, couldn't speak. He just stood there silently screaming at his knees, because they'd picked this day, of all days, to not want to work right anymore. He was so busy thinking about the wire and his knees now that it only registered once he'd already left the house that he hadn't spoken a word to his wife.

They had to go see Tony at his dad's place today, which presented several problems. Tony kept having heart attacks, making him tense and beady-eyed like a rabbit. He wasn't a barrel of laughs on an ordinary day; now he acted like he might die any second. So this week, instead of going up to the back of the butcher shop, Tony made them meet at his father's mansion in Livingston. It would be Marty's first time there wearing a wire.

The place creeped them all out, Marty most of all. The chill crept over you as soon as you drove up to the ornate gates, flanked by lions as big as the New York Public Library's, probably stolen from somewhere just like that. In his younger days, Richie the Boot's one relatively legitimate business had been in wrecking and salvage; he'd spent 30 years going out to get statuary and bring it back to his his vast, fantastical, Transylvanian five-bedroom house.

When you went to a museum or something, the statues were a soft white or creamy colored, but Richie's looked like some kid had gone crazy and painted everything. The gates were brown and green stone flecked with red. Broken mosaics of garish maroons and blues flanked every statue, most of which carried signs in stone letters telling you what they were, as though Richie didn't trust anybody to figure that kind of thing out for themselves. There were man-sized gargoyles with Medusa heads, Venuses with broken arms and chunks carved out of their bodies like attack victims, and a weird man-beast with horns and the body of an elk or something. It was a nuthouse of a place.

Today Marty rode in the passenger seat with Johnno, who was driving. Johnno was a young associate, Ralphie's nephew. The two men pulled up to the gate, staring straight ahead as they waited for it to creak open. He mentally prepared for Richie's henchmen, who would appear spontaneously from their secret guard post hidey-holes, cradling machine guns like babies, and stare Johnno and Marty down like they were killers from another planet.

Once the guards let you in, on the long paved drive up to the house, you had to keep staring straight ahead. You didn't want to look back over the hill, back in that dark part of the yard where the cement fire pit was. It was actually a crematorium, eight feet wide, filled with men's ashes. Marty had been to it a few times before, in the dead of night, on body disposal duty. Sometimes when you got near the pit, the wind would pick up its ashes and they would fly in your face. He hadn't had to go near it in the last couple of years, but knowing he was close by gave him chills.

"D'ya hear about what happened up there the other night, Marty?"

Marty realized in that second that whatever he said next would be his first words that day, caught on the wire. He could barely speak, just shrugged his shoulders and muttered.

"They brought that little guy up there, you know, Solly's guy? Hit him with a shovel so hard it woulda killed an ox. But the guy wouldn't go down. He just thrashed around like a fish on a boat!"

Johnno drove slowly, as they he was trying to delay arriving at Richie's house, shaking his head and chuckling in that nervous way they all did whenever they had to come up here.

"Tony thought he'd go fast because he was so small, right? Took 'em like an hour. Then his wife's all up his ass because he's late for dinner."

Marty thought wildly for a second about what to say. Then, before he could check his response, it shot out of him.

"As little as they are," he said, "they struggle."

Marty ran a hand over his face and spent the next few seconds on a vision of Johnny just driving the car off the drive and over the hill, up to the lip of the pit, and dumping him in.

Then a sharp pain in his chest. It started as almost a pinprick sensation, then grew and grew in seconds to take his breath away. He felt his arms pinned to his sides, dead weights of pain. His felt his eyes bug out.

But he also felt strangely calm about it all, calm for the first time in months. He thought — not necessarily in words, but in pulsing red and purple images bumping around in his brain — that this must be what it felt like for Tony. This must be what it felt like to die of a heart attack.

16

James Cash didn't show up for work after the riots. So once things were quiet, once the shopkeepers had started to board up the windows and close up their stores for good, once the secretaries started feeling safe in City Hall again, Donnie went to the Hayes Homes after work to see him.

James answered the door, the sound of the TV evening news behind him. He said nothing. He stepped back and swung the door wide so Donnie could see Fred and Inez, sitting on the couch in front of the fan, watching the TV.

They shook hands. Donnie asked James if he planned to come back to work. James said no, offered Donnie some iced tea and a seat near the TV.

"This is my mother, Inez, and my brother Fred," he said, walking Donnie over to the couch. To them, he said: "This is Donnie. He was my boss in the mayor's office."

Inez half-stood to shake Donnie's hand, then sat back down, and Fred nodded at him. Nobody knew what to say. There was a commercial on for toothpaste, so they watched that, silently.

Finally James came back with the iced tea, sat in the chair next to Donnie and said, "they say it's fine to go outside now, everything's over.

But she," he nodded at his mother, "wants us here."

"It was bad," Fred said to Donnie as though they were old friends, when in fact they'd never met before. "People were going crazy."

Donnie just nodded, trying to relax into being accepted here, drinking his tea. He looked at Inez and Fred on the couch, James on a chair, looking at the TV, and realized they'd been sitting in those same spots for most of the last week.

The WNEW TV news showed pictures of National Guard jeeps and tanks, of Negroes running through the streets. Then the anchorman was interviewing the mayor again for something like the fourth time in five days. His first question was why Negro applicants hadn't been given more jobs in the Addonizio administration.

"I have given them jobs in my administration," Addonizio responded, hooded lids shading tired-looking eyes.

The grey-haired, chisel-faced newsman waited a beat, then said, "but your critics charge that those jobs have been very slow in coming."

The mayor nodded, as though he'd been expecting the question.

"The Negroes are not content to grow their situation slowly and moderately," he said. "They want the whole ball game."

Donnie didn't know what to look at. He couldn't look at the Cashes. It made him want to vomit to look at the TV, but he kept looking at the TV.

Bob Walker came on next. The newscaster asked him about the CORE demonstration outside City Hall back in the spring. He laid it out: when the key job in the Newark School System opened up in the spring, Addonizio passed over Budget Director Wilbur Parker, a black man, and appointed Councilman James T. Callahan, his uneducated white crony. Parker was a CPA with a bachelor's degree; Callahan held a high-school diploma.

"I don't understand," Fred said. "Why are they talking about this now? This is old news. The National Guard was here. The Guard! They brought guns here they didn't even know how to use. They were killing people just walking to the store!"

Inez put a hand on his knee and gave him a look.

"And who told you that? Did you see that for yourself?"

"No ma'am," Fred frowned. "You didn't let me out of the house."

"You didn't see it for yourself, you don't know for sure what you're talking about," she said sharply, with a glance at Donnie.

Donnie didn't know how to answer any of this, or if he was expected to join in the conversation at all.

But James said, "It all connects, Fred. The school board thing, the medical school, the police trying to take people out for no reason. It all adds up."

Then James took a breath, leaned forward and looked his brother in the eye.

"But that there," he said, pointing to the TV, "that's a white newsman there, trying to understand."

Fred looked to Donnie like a hothead who was trying to hold himself back, but he didn't answer that way. He just nodded, and he said, "All right."

Donnie started to wonder what the hell he was doing in the Cashes' apartment. He wanted badly to point out the obvious: that he knew it too, that everything had connected and added up in the fire and death that had gone on outside for the last six days. He wanted to point out that he understood it too, but what did it matter now? He thought he'd have a stilted conversation with James, make sure he and his family were okay, and then leave. Now here he was in the middle of everything.

He felt a sense of time splitting, a sense of nothing happening yet too much going on, all at the same time. When he stepped into the office tomorrow morning there would be people streaming everywhere, all talking at once, everybody wanting something and putting out a heated energy that would carry him through the whole day, through lunch and dinner without a spare second to think. And yet tonight in this apartment, there was just this family, and fresh air from the fan. And he still couldn't keep up.

They sat watching TV for awhile. Donnie wanted to leave, but didn't know how. Then Fred seemed to realize who he was, and why he was there. He leaned forward, clasped his hands and rested his arms on his knees.

"You work for Addonizio?"

"I do."

"So what do you do exactly?"

Donnie took a big breath.

"I'm the administrative assistant," he said. "I organize the day-to-day activities for the mayor's office. I work with other governmental organizations, and handle scheduling and special projects, things like that."

"Do you think...." Fred began, then stopped, then started again: "Does the mayor understand what happened this week? Do you think he knows?"

Donnie took another big breath.

"You have to understand, the mayor's office is answerable to so many different people," he began, slipping into government-speak. "Anytime there is violence, City Hall has to react in a very prescribed way. There's no time to figure out why it's happening, you just have to do what you can to stop it. In this case, people rioting and looting stores in the middle of the night, there's not much you can even do to stop it.... You just feel frustrated."

Fred seemed to accept this, to let Donnie have his moment. Inez and James watched Fred intently. He nodded.

"Yes, but do you think he knows?" he asked again. "Does he understand why?"

Fred was asking about Hugh, not him, but Donnie felt his own conscience being interrogated. He wanted to pour out everything, how naive he felt, how unwittingly destructive. How he was a public health guy, always had been, that's what he went to school for, and how he'd fallen so in love with the idea of a new medical school steps from downtown that he was willing to overlook the 500 families who were going to have to move to make it all happen. How Clara had gone back to stay with her parents the day after the riots started and hadn't been back since, how he knew she felt culpable as a dependable employee of Santoro's and how she wasn't planning on going back to her job anymore, either.

But they didn't want to hear that. They wanted to hear whether he thought the mayor knew what he was doing.

"I don't really know," he finally said, looking at the floor. "I can't tell."

June 1969

17

When Gloria's doctor used the word "catatonia," it sounded to her like a lovely island in Italy. She wondered for a half-second whether Catatonia was near Naples, if it was somewhere she might go when this was all over.

But he'd meant catatonic. Her friends had brought her to the doctor the day after she'd sat through the first day of her husband's trial on corruption charges in federal court. She'd sat through the proceedings like a robot, like a statue, watching and listening, turned to stone.

It started when it really hit her that her husband was trial, there on the stand, refusing to answer questions about anything but his own name. Nine other men were named to criminal charges with Hugh, but she didn't know most of them. She just knew her husband.

"State your name?"

"Hugh Addonizio."

"State your position?"

"I refuse to answer on the grounds that it may incriminate me."

"You refuse to state your position?"

"I refuse to answer on the grounds that it may incriminate me."

"Are you the elected mayor of Newark, New Jersey?"

"I refuse to answer on the grounds that it may incriminate me."

"You refuse to confirm or deny that you are the elected mayor of Newark?"

"I refuse to answer on the grounds that it may incriminate me."

The catatonia actually happened right in there somewhere. Gloria could remember how that conversation between her husband and the prosecutor had gotten started, but then things got hazy.

She'd spent the days before the trial started reading the report of what they called a "blue-ribbon" commission appointed to study the riots. Her husband's quotes had been laid out there at length, and to her he seemed reasonable, even sure of himself during the hours of interviews they'd made him submit to as they tried to get to the bottom of what happened.

The report was a blow-by-blow of what had been happening to Hugh downtown during the six days of rioting, while she'd stayed home in New Shrewsbury making the children sandwiches and listening to the news on the radio in the kitchen.

The report's writers had let Hugh come off pretty well, at first. His first quote about how and why the riots had broken out made a lot of sense to her:

"It's not so hard to understand," he'd told them. "The material was there in terms of problems in housing, education and the effects of generations of neglect and bigotry. The atmosphere was right, because of mistakes, because of misunderstandings, and because of the insanity of a few misguided fools who believe riots are a healthy exercise for America."

But then the report spiraled down into who said and did what on those days and nights, hour by hour. Whoever wrote it seemed determine to lay out the detail of every single call Hugh made and what he said, if only so that the commission members could try to catch Hugh in mistakes and half-truths. The report painstakingly detailed the date and time of every single instance either Hugh or Dominic Santoro told newsmen the violence seemed to be ending, when in fact there was renewed shooting and fires within minutes of their speaking the words. Still: could her husband really be blamed for hoping the violence would end? Was it really supposed to be his fault that people kept killing each other?

Then there were accounts of those days that made her think twice. Hugh had told her that Governor Warren had made the decision, on Thursday, July 12, the first day of the riots, to call in the National Guard. Guardsmen showed up on Friday night and were then blamed for at least a portion of the deaths overall. But the report said the mayor didn't ask for the National Guard until early Friday morning, in a frantic phone call to Governor Warren.

The finger-pointing went on and on through the commission report. Reading it made Gloria nauseous. Finally she read: "Mayor Addonizio felt that, 'during the whole course of this thing I was sort of left out of a lot of things that were going on, and this is my city and I have to stay here after the people pull out.' The Governor observed, however, that Mayor Addonizio 'almost completely withdrew from the sharing of any direction of this situation.'"

Still, after setting the report down weeks ago, after Hugh told her he had been indicted on corruption charges, after she'd watched him head downtown for meeting after meeting with lawyers and detectives, how could she possibly have ended up watching him on the stand in federal court, watching them call him a defendant, calling the case The United States v. Addonizio?

She vaguely remembered Hugh's new lawyer, Tom O'Reilley, finding her in the courtroom just before things got started. He said the prosecuting attorneys were going to try to to prove that Hugh got his friends construction contracts without going through the proper channels. That undercover agents had secretly taped her husband and his friends' phone calls and meetings, and now had hours and hours of them talking about crooked business dealings and mob hits. They said the words extortion, kickback and conspiracy a lot, but they never defined them. They said Tony Boy Boiardo was supposed to be there on the stand too, but he was in the hospital recovering from a heart attack. And people were saying that Martin Attunale, Lila's husband, should have stood trial for murder. But he was dead now.

Her mother-in-law sat next to her in the courtroom while her daughter watched the younger children back at home. And there sat her husband, on the stand looking like a chastised boy, refusing to admit he was the mayor of Newark.

She was in Catatonia the whole time, as men took the stand looking dour and testified about what they did or did not do wrong as it pertained to city building contracts. It seemed like so much fuss, so many words, all about nothing. She was there as the defendants were finally sentenced, and her husband got ten years. She sat there like a stone while her mother-in-law burst into tears and started to wail.

She didn't keep any newspaper accounts of that time; she tried not to read them at all. Later all she would remember of the trial was how she'd gotten this ridiculous, fleeting idea of Catatonia in her mind, this remote Italian island where they'd all go on vacation someday.

July 1974

Epilogue

They sent Hugh away to federal prison for 10 years, but O'Reilley worked the whole time on appeals, one after the other, and got him out in five. They sent him home to her, with vague threats he'd have to go back soon if he lost the latest appeal. He took up training homing pigeons in the backyard, never going into the city at all.

One day in the summer, she was in the kitchen, the children were at school and he was out in the backyard with the birds. O'Reilley called with the good news: Their appeal was successful. No more prison.

He came into the kitchen while she was still holding the phone to the side of her head.

"You're free," she told him. "You're free!"

Acknowledgements

Thank you Rob Rushin, Judy Rushin, Laura Barge O'Sullivan, Tom DePlonty, Karen Barry, Lincoln Jones, Ashley McNeal, Caitlin Oliver-Gans, Anne-Marie Littenberg, Jessica Nelson, Ellen Powell, Diane Roberts, Kate Sykes, Linda Hall, Richard Brunck, Kim Round, Jenny Milchman, Diana Jones-Ellis, Barry Ray, Jeffrey Seay, Michelle Dustin, Ann Morris, David Morris, Beth Round, Kim Addonizio, Andrea Brecheen, Mark Pudlow, Kati Schardl, Leisa Pichard, Kim MacQueen, Judy Round, Christy "Cho" Womack, Erika Nichols, Ashley Ivey, Angela Palm, Peter Biello, Jason Lewis, Eileen Drennan and Jonathan Lammers. Your help made this book possible.

Thanks to my dad, Fred Addonizio. Thanks to my writing group friends, especially Kate Sykes, Angela Palm, Jessica Nelson, Patrick Dodge, Niels Reinhardt, Erica Nichols, Peter Biello and Alan Uris. Thanks Cindy Barnes for being a supportive friend and my partner in publishing. Thanks Steve and Claire MacQueen for your editorial eyes. Thank you Martin Simpson for beautiful design. Thanks to Kim Round, Richard Brunck, Leisa Pichard, Tim Brookes and everybody else who encouraged this book by listening to me prattle on about mayoral politics and the NJ mafia between 2007-2014.

www.ingramcontent.com/pod-product-compliance
Lightning Source LLC
Chambersburg PA
CBHW051305250626
47155CB00009B/3436